Before I
Let Go

Other books by Kimberly T. Matthews

Promise You Won't Tell Nobody

Fruit of My Womb

The Perfect Shoe

Ninety-Nine and a Half Just Won't Do

A Little Hurt Ain't Never Hurt Nobody (Fall 2008)

Before I
Let Go

Kimberly T. Matthews

URBAN BOOKS

http://www.urbanbooks.net

This is a work of fiction. Any references or similarities to actual events, real people, living or dead, or to real locales are intended to give the novel a sense of reality. Any similarity in other names, characters, places, and incidents is entirely coincidental.

URBAN SOUL is published by

Urban Books
1199 Straight Path
West Babylon, NY 11704

ISBN-13: 978-1-59983-056-8
ISBN-10: 1-59983-056-8

First Printing: March 2008

10 9 8 7 6 5 4 3 2 1

Printed in the United States of America

Dedicated to the One I'm never letting go of . . .

From the Journal of Micah P. Abraham

A man never can tell how a woman is going to react when the man she loves has gotten on her very last nerve. The very last. "I'm sorry, baby," is not gonna work anymore. Neither will, "I love you, baby; you're the woman of my dreams." Nope, she's heard it all before and it won't work anymore because he's messed up for the last time.

Now, some women will try to fight. That's not such a great idea. If a woman recognizes her own strengths and weaknesses—and generally we're pretty weak in comparison to men—trying to fight a man is simply not in our best interest. Yet, there are a few sistahs who will land a blow or two when they've reached their limit. The other thing about that, though, is hitting somebody might land you in jail if he uses his brain and calls the cops. Even worse, it could land you a broken jaw, a black eye, and some other stuff if he decides to use his fists instead.

Some women will break up stuff when they've had enough. You know, the man comes home and his living room is completely trashed because the girl took to it with a hammer? That works best in videos. A woman could go to jail behind that too, so it's not recommended.

Now, we as women should have a lot more self-esteem than to sit around feeling sorry for ourselves and start singing "I'm Going Down" 'cause he ain't around. That shouldn't be happening. Neither should we put an orange in a sock and slug ourselves in the face, then call the cops and blame it on him. Personally, I'm far too beautiful to intentionally compromise my looks.

Well, it's August 5th, I'm officially fed up, and y'all know what R. Kelly says: when a woman's fed up, it ain't nothing you can do about it. But there is just one thing that I just gotta do before I let go.

Micah and Erin

"But he said he bought them for me last year," Erin exclaimed as she pulled the last straight pin from the material she had draped around Micah's shoulders.

"And all I'm saying is I've owned a lot of panties in my twenty-five years, and I have never not recognized my own draws." Micah's words casually tumbled out of her mouth as she stepped down from the stool she'd been standing on for the past hour and plopped down on the couch with the TV remote. She began flipping through channels, taking no care that she was only clad in a strapless bra and a pair of boy-leg briefs. "Can you hand me those Doritos off the counter in the kitchen?" She never even looked at Erin again, although Erin stood in the middle of the living room with one hand on her hip and the other holding an undone coat hanger with a black and yellow lace thong hanging off its end.

Erin stomped off toward the kitchen, pulled a thirty-gallon trash bag from a cabinet beneath the sink, deposited the hanger and the panties, then leaned back against the counter with her arms folded against her chest. "Let's see," she spoke loud enough for Micah to hear but really talked out loud for her own benefit. "Gideon got me a digital camera for my birthday . . . three new suits for work when I got that promotion . . . a few mini gifts in between that and Christmas . . . these panties just aren't registering." She pressed her lips together, realizing Micah had a point. After all, Erin currently had about a hundred pairs of panties and could give an account for every single pair. *Even the ones that I've bought and have never even worn before,* she thought.

"Bring a cup of ice too . . . please," Micah called from the living room.

"How is it that I'm trying to have a crisis here and all you can be concerned about is a bag of chips, a cup of ice, and the doggone cooking channel?"

"Because I don't have man issues right now, so I'm not going to let myself get stressed out over someone else's man issues."

"You could at least act like you care." Erin practically threw the bag of chips at her girlfriend.

"I do care. I already told you what to do; tell that busta to get to steppin'."

Erin sighed. "It's just not that easy."

"Why not? I don't see what's so hard about it. Those were not your panties, he's sleeping with someone else, and in your bed at that." Micah shrugged as she threw her head back and filled her mouth with crushed ice. "Shoahlim shayines'," she mumbled. "Moofon."

"What?"

Micah waited a minute until the bits of ice

melted, then repeated herself. "So all I'm saying is move on. It's just that simple. If he's cheating on you, then he's not treating you like a queen, and you are a queen, right?"

"Of course I am," Erin muttered as she slumped on the couch and sighed.

"Well act like it then."

"Okay but—"

"Hold on a minute," Micah interrupted as she raised the television's volume level.

"Before placing your dessert on the plate, simply place a paper doily on it first, spray it lightly with a nonstick cooking spray, sift cocoa mixed with a little cinnamon on a white plate, or powdered sugar if you're using a colored plate." The show's host demonstrated for a studio audience and his home viewers as he spoke. "Then carefully lift the doily, and there you have it—a beautifully decorated serving plate for your favorite dessert. You can even try stenciling the top of your deserts for a wonderful match."

"That was pretty; I should do that for the cake plates." Micah jumped to her feet and snapped her fingers. "Ooh, I meant to show you the programs I ordered." She dug through her tote and pulled out a small package. "These came yesterday," she said excitedly. "Rossi hasn't seen them yet, but he's pretty much letting me pick everything out anyway."

Erin took a single sheet of the unfolded paper and admired the calla lily with its ribbon-wrapped stem. "These are nice. I just can't believe Rossi isn't taking an active part in the planning."

"He's planning the honeymoon." Micah took the sheet back from her friend and placed it back in the box with the others. "Plus men don't know anything about planning weddings anyway."

"It seems like he's being a little nonchalant about the whole thing. You don't even have your ring yet, and here you are planning and purchasing stuff."

"That's because the ring I want costs twelve thousand dollars." Micah lifted her brows knowingly. "I don't mind waiting a minute for him to save a few more dollars to get it for me."

"Suppose he doesn't get that one?"

"Oh, he's gonna get it. You know why? Because I'm a queen and he knows you bring the queen what she wants."

"Okay, when he comes rolling in here with something he got out the Crackerjack box, let's see how much of a queen you'll be."

"Anyway!" Micah dismissed. "Are you still going to be able to go with me on Saturday to look at headpieces?

"Bright and early, but for right now I need to go to bed so I can be ready in the morning for this zoo we call work."

"You're just going to put me out, huh?"

"You know what they say: you ain't got to go home but . . ."

"Yeah, yeah, yeah, I know the rest. Let me just get dressed real quick." Micah giggled as she pulled a pair of sweats and a baby T-shirt from a small tote bag and pulled them both on. "I'll see you tomorrow. Let me get my thirty minutes in before I get home."

As Micah pulled out of Erin's driveway, she thought about Erin's words. If she was honest with herself, she'd see that Rossi had been pretty standoffish about their wedding plans. Each time she had brought up new ideas, he'd listened but offered little to no response. Micah thought it a little strange but pushed it out of her mind each time and pressed forward with her planning. As long as Rossi showed up at the alter, things would be fine.

The parking lot in front of Curves seemed to be more crowded than normal. After a few seconds of circling the lot, Micah pulled into a vacant spot and trotted inside. As she completed her warm-up and made her way through the circuit training equipment, she mentally reviewed her wedding checklist. Although she had been pricked more times than a few, her dress was coming along very nicely. It would be an Emma Scott lookalike, but who would know, other than her wallet not having to come up with $2,500. Erin was making the gown for practically free. The park had been reserved for under $50 and was a perfect backdrop for a spring ceremony. The chairs and tents had been reserved and the invites picked out. She smiled as she forced her legs forward, pushing the weight of the leg press away from her body, but then a frown began to take over her face. Glancing down at her still empty finger, she was more than perturbed that Rossi, though he had asked her hand in marriage, was seemingly taking his time putting a ring on her finger. She tried to be patient; the ring she really wanted did cost a pretty penny, and with Rossi being a store manager for Chick-fil-A his pockets weren't shallow, but neither were they deep. Nonetheless Micah believed she was well worth every dime he'd save up for the ring's purchase and they'd find other ways to cut corners on the actual wedding itself, as she was so skillfully doing.

"Give him a little more time," she huffed, jogging in place between a set of machines. "But he ain't got forever," she added, recognizing her own doubts about her finger being bare. "And if he takes too long, I'ma have to let him go."

Romni and Charvette

Romni rolled over on her right side coming breath to breath with her boyfriend, T-Dog. His real name was Clarence Cleotus Tyndale but he'd hated the name since his formative years, and as soon as he grew the first hair on his chin, he felt T-Dog better suited him, which couldn't have been closer to the truth.

How did I get myself in this mess? Romni thought after staring at T-Dog's sleeping face for a full minute. She sighed as she pulled herself from the bed, then stepped on a condom wrapper on the way to the bathroom. She lightly touched her face with her fingertips as she looked at the small bruise that was the evidence of the slap she'd taken the night before when she'd lied about her tip money. No matter what she did to hide her earnings from T-Dog, he seemed to always know when she'd skimmed a few dollars off the top for herself. Last night, he'd wanted more beer, which had prompted his request for cash.

"I already gave you all I had," she'd answered.

"I'ma ask you one more . . ." Instead of ending his sentence with the word *time*, T-Dog landed a slap so powerful that Romni spun to the bedroom floor practically before she had realized what had happened. Fighting back tears, she swiftly dug into the pocket of her bra that was made for holding removable padding and pulled out her last twenty dollars and raised her shaking arm to hand the money to T-Dog.

In no rush, he took a long drag from a cigarette, then stooped down to meet her eye to eye. "Next time you see fit to lie to me"—he had pulled the cigarette from his lips and jabbed toward her face—"I'ma put your eye out." Romni kept silent as she stared at the glowing end of the tobacco stick. T-Dog plucked the money from her fingers; stood and adjusted his pants, which hung well below his waist and hips; and headed for the door. "Have me som'na eat by the time I get back." The door slammed behind him and the sound of silence settled in her government-subsidized-housing apartment.

Another ten minutes passed with Romni hugging her knees to her chest and resting her chin atop them both, allowing the slow trickle of tears to roll down her face and trail down her shins. In that ten minutes, both everything and nothing ran through her mind so quickly that she could barely keep up.

Everything included her thoughts of getting out of the rut she'd found herself in, leaving

T-Dog, leaving the projects, leaving her job at the greasy hole-in-the-wall she worked at frying chicken and waiting tables. Nothing included what she felt she had in her favor to make that happen. After three years of living with T-Dog, her strength was zeroed down to nothing, her self-esteem was nonexistent, and she felt she lacked the education to make herself more marketable in the workplace. She'd secretly been trying to save money to run away from it all, but with T-Dog taking every dollar she earned, she seemed to be in a catch-22. There was always Rossi, who had helped his sister before by giving her cash, paying her incredibly minimal (yet behind) rent and a few other bills, but once he became aware of Romni allowing T-Dog to live with her sans employment, he wasn't as generous. Maybe he would let her come stay with him—at least for a little while—until T-Dog found another woman to lay up under. *The worst thing he could say to me is no,* she thought, twisting her lips. She'd make a point to call him within the next week.

Knowing that T-Dog would return in another thirty minutes or so, Romni pulled one of his wifebeaters over her head and slipped a pair of sweatpants over her boy shorts before heading to the kitchen. Using a pack of Ramen Noodles and a frozen hamburger patty, a little dried onion, and some tomato sauce, she cooked up what she called spaghetti; piled it on a plate; placed a couple slices of processed, prewrapped cheese on top; then took the dish to her back door and set it on the porch adjacent to the trash can, then stepped back into her apartment. She watched from the screened doorway as flies hovered and landed on the meal in a matter of seconds, covering the food as it were a soiled diaper. Romni let the plate sit out while she went back to the kitchen, dropped cubes of ice in a glass, then added orange soda and sipped slowly. After several minutes, she sat the glass on the small glass-top table in her dining area, went to the back door, shooed the flies, brought T-Dog's meal back in, and covered it with plastic wrap before sticking it in the microwave to warm it up a bit.

She smirked to herself, but then nearly threw up in the kitchen sink thinking of the filth that now covered the food, coming to the realization that after T-Dog ate, he would demand sex from her. In an instant she thought to fake a yeast infection, which would mean he wouldn't want her at all, or he would use a condom. She knew he wasn't sensitive enough to kiss her, but she hadn't thought about oral sex. "Just please don't want a blow job," she said to herself, regretting her actions. Her hand raised to feel along her jawline, remembering the punch he'd landed there two days before. "I'll just say I can't open my mouth good," Romni whispered.

Hearing the sound of a key being slid into the lock, she hurriedly removed T-Dog's dinner, jabbed a fork into it, and set it on the table. "That's what I'm talkin' 'bout," he commented as he inhaled the aroma of cooked food. Within minutes, he gobbled down the tainted provisions while he gulped a few beers. Then he watched a video of barely clad women dancing for dollar bills while he jerked on his manhood until he released, and then collapsed in slumber. It was a few hours later when he'd stumbled to bed, awoke Romni from her sleep, and attempted to ram his way inside her from behind.

Before he made his entry, Romni begged him to use a condom, blurting out her feigned infection. He slurred a few obscenities but obliged, found satisfaction within two minutes, then went back to sleep.

Not wanting to be in her own home any longer than she had to, Romni washed up at the sink, brushed her teeth and hair, then reached for her panties and T-shirt, which hung over the shower curtain rod. The shirt was still slightly damp from being hand washed the night before, but by the time she pressed out some of the dampness with the iron and walked to the restaurant in the hot sun, she'd be dry as a bone. Quietly she tiptoed around the house as she dressed, gently lifted her keys from the table, and sneaked out her front door.

A temporary sense of relief washed over her once she eased the door closed and began her stride down the sidewalk, thanking God for life, health, and strength. It was something that Josephine Evans had instilled in both her children from the time they began leaving the house for school. As she did most mornings, Romni added a little more on to her prayer. "Lord, please help me to change my situation. Help my mind to be transformed so that I can think straight and figure out how to get myself together. You created me and you let me live, so you must see something in me worth keeping around. Help me to see it too, Lord. If I can see what you see, then I can be what you have called me to be. But right now, God, my vision is all jacked up and I need you to help me with that." Just then Romni's cell phone buzzed, interrupting her prayer. "In Jesus's name I pray, amen," she blurted before answering. "Hey, Ma."

"Hey, baby," Josephine started. "You still coming by here today? I have had my mouth fixed for gizzards all week, and I need a couple of things from the store."

"I'ma try to come by there when I get off work if it's not too late," Romni replied, glancing at the time displayed on her wrist.

"How you holding up?"

"I'm all right," she answered, while her mind transitioned to the grown, unemployed man she'd left lying in her bed.

"You sure? You know I don't like you . . ."

"Yeah, Ma, I know. You done told me at least fifty times you don't like Clarence living in my house, and you don't like the way he treats me," she finished for her mother, then paused pensively. "Ma?"

"Hmm?"

"I'm thinking about . . ." Romni bit into her lower lip, not quite sure what she was thinking about at all. Once she formulated a few words in her mind, she continued. "I'm thinking 'bout asking Rossi if I could come stay with him for a little while."

"You gone take that boy with you? 'Cause if you are, ain't no need in you going nowhere."

"No, Ma. Do you always have to be so . . . so mean about it?" she huffed, much rather wanting her mother's support than her judgment and ridicule.

"I'm just telling you before you go down there being a burden on your brother. If you gonna leave, leave, baby, but make sure when you leave . . . leave! Don't do like Lot's wife and turn around looking at the mess you left behind. She looked back and met her destruction. You remember that?"

"Yes, ma'am," Romni sighed. "Right now I'm just thinking about it, Ma. I don't know what I might do."

"Well you need to hurry up and do something. I told you that pea-headed boy wasn't worth a nickel when you came bringing him up in my house years ago," Josephine continued.

Romni massaged her temple as she listened to her mother's reprimand. "You're right, Ma," she said in an attempt to end the call. "I should have listened to you then. I'm at work now so I gotta go," she lied, still having four blocks to walk before she'd be at Big Bubba's Buffet. "I'll come by later; love you." Before Josephine could respond, Romni pushed the end button and jammed the phone back into the pocket of her jeans, but suddenly reminded herself that she had not given her mother the opportunity to say what things she needed from the store. "I'll call back later," she spoke to herself, needing some time to digest what Josephine had said for the umpteenth time.

She knew her mother was right. She just hadn't found a way to let go.

Charvette looked out her living room window for the tenth time. Kinston was late again, if he would show at all. Although this very thing had happened more times than Charvette could even count, it always left her feeling empty, a feeling she could never get used to. Nonetheless, she stood clad in a black BCBG draped tunic dress and a pair of red stilettos waiting for his arrival.

Exhaling a heavy sigh, she found herself trekking to the bathroom to check her appearance again, regardless of the fact that she knew she looked perfect. She turned slowly in front of the full-length mirror, appreciating the length of her legs and her curvaceous figure through the jersey-knit material. Her eyes traveled up her body from her manicured toes to her freshly texturized crown of glory. "It's a shame for one woman to be this fine," she commented out loud as she smiled to herself.

Thinking she heard a car pulling up in front of her house, Charvette jetted back to the window and peered through the blinds only to be disappointed. She seated herself in her favorite chair and jammed her hand between the cushion and the chair's side and pulled up a small journal. She opened to a blank page, dug a pen out of her purse, and began to record her thoughts.

> *Here I sit alone . . . again*
> *Waiting on a married man*
> *He says he loves me more than life*
> *But can he when he has a wife?*
> *Am I desperate, am I scared?*
> *Am I content with a lover shared?*
> *A love so wrong*
> *But a love so strong*
> *That it just keeps on keeping on*

Stuffing the journal back into its crevice, Charvette leaned back and sighed again as she tried to remind herself of her justifiable reasons for dating Kinston Barnes. When they met, he wasn't even with his wife, which in Charvette's book made him fair game. He was sitting at the blackjack table at Dover Downs Hotel and Casino with the favor of lady luck when he and Charvette first caught eyes. Kinston's tongue peeked through his mouth and quickly licked his bottom lip as he absorbed her thick five-foot-ten frame, casually dressed in a white linen Capri pantsuit, contrasted by a lace black shell and peep-toe wedged heel sandals.

Kinston spoke no words but kept his eyes on her, watching her saunter over to a section of dollar slots and take a seat. Minutes later he approached, drink in hand.

"Excuse me," he started. Charvette acknowledged him with only a glance as she smoothed a crinkled twenty-dollar bill over her thigh and attempted to feed it into the machine a third time. "I got that for you, sweetheart." Before she could protest, Kinston slid a hundred-dollar bill into the slot. "If you win more than a hundred dollars, you have to agree to have dinner with me." He took a few steps back toward the table where he'd been seated while he let his eyes roam her profile. "I'll be right over there." He nodded with his head. "Let me know what you win."

Kinston had picked up several women, single and married, with that tactic and found that his financial investment always paid huge dividends in more ways than one. His strategy once again proved successful when thirty minutes later Charvette approached him with a huge grin and a cash-out ticket worth more than $800.

"How'd you do?" he asked once she reached his side.

Charvette glanced down at his hand in search of

a wedding band but didn't find one. "I think I owe you a dinner date."

"So you won a little something, huh?" he asked, smoothing two fingers over his moustache, flashing a smile, then looking down at his cards.

"Just a little bit," she smirked, looking into his deep-set coal-black eyes, accented with thick brows.

"Give me a minute here." While Kinston finished his last hand, Charvette took notice of his other features. Wesley Snipes–colored skin housed his well-defined muscles, and his hair was neatly cut into a temple fade. Dressed in Purple Label Ralph Lauren pants and a matching polo, he collected chips from his winning hand and stood to his feet. He smiled again at Charvette and said, "I'm ready." Then he added, "I'm Kinston, by the way," as he slid his hands into his pants pockets.

"Kinston," she repeated. "Nice name. I'm Charvette."

"Unique name for a unique woman," he said, looking directly into her eyes, causing her to blush.

"Thanks." They took a few steps in silence. "You come here often?" she asked, not knowing what else to say.

"Mmm," he pondered for a second. "They kinda know my name around here, I think." He chuckled. "What about you?"

"I was actually on my way to New York for a few days to do a little shopping but took a detour," she confessed. "I thought I'd try my luck to see if I could make me a few extra shopping dollars."

"How's your luck been?" His eyes floated from her oval face down to the curve of her breasts then back up again.

"Oh, it was *well* worth the stop," she exclaimed, with a giggle. "I'm ready to do a little damage now. Thanks, by the way," she said, digging into her purse and pulling out five twenties to offer back to him.

"You can keep that," he dismissed as they took a seat in a booth at Festival Buffet.

"Why did you do that anyway?"

Kinston shrugged. "I saw a beautiful woman whom I wanted to talk to, and if I would have just said, ''Scuse me, what's your name?' you wouldn't have given me the time of day."

"So you've tried this before, then?"

"Actually no, but since luck was being a lady all night tonight, I thought I'd keep it working. And like everything else I've tried this evening, I seem to have come up with another winning hand." Charvette blushed again. "Have I?" he asked, seeking confirmation that she would entertain him that night.

"Why don't we grab something to eat," she suggested, with a sly grin.

Over a scrumptious selection of fresh soups, salads, slow-roasted carved meats, Asian and Italian dishes, all-you-can-eat crab legs and other seafood, pizza choices, and desserts, the two spent the next hour and a half chatting and getting to know each other.

"Where are you from?" Charvette asked between chews.

"Fredericksburg. And you?"

"I live in Richmond. What are you doing here by yourself?" Charvette asked.

"Just needed some time away, I guess."

"Time away from what—work, home, school, kids, *prison*?" She guffawed.

"From my soon-to-be ex-wife, who's driving me up the wall," he revealed. It was the first mention of his marital status.

Charvette couldn't help but gasp as she felt a certain uneasiness settle in the pit of her stomach. She cleared her throat slightly before she spoke. "You're married?"

"Only because my divorce is not final . . . yet." He bit into his lower lip, studying her face for reaction.

"So while you're sitting here with me, you have a wife sitting at home, probably wondering where you are," Charvette shot across the table, uncovering the onset of fury.

"Trust me, wherever Naomi is, she is certainly not thinking about me," he huffed and shook his head. "I am the very last thing she's thinking about."

"Right," she responded in sarcastic disbelief.

Kinston shook his head as he stirred his spoon in a pool of melting ice cream. "Seriously, Charvette. That relationship is so dead."

"But you're not divorced . . . 'yet,' as you put it. That's so typical of married men," she said, irritated.

"We've not been together in two years, but she won't sign the papers," he explained. "She wants me to fork over a ton of money first, and I've been less than willing to do that."

"Yeah, yeah, yeah. Let me see your hands." With crinkled brows expressing confusion, Kinston extended both his hands toward Charvette. Right away, she grabbed his left hand and studied his ring finger intently for discoloration of his skin, or a grooved impression left by a band, but his finger was smooth and unmarked. "Hmph!"

she commented, pushing his hand away. "What do you do for a living anyway?"

"I'm a senior research chemist for a pharmaceutical company."

Although it was words he spoke, what rang in Charvette's hearing was the imaginary sound of millions of quarters being released from a slot machine. *Jackpot! This brother is paid!* she kept to herself. *But he has a wife. Damn!*

"I don't have anything to hide," he said, showing his palms were empty as if he were performing a magic trick.

"I don't date married men," Charvette said flatly. "Thanks for dinner," she ended, rising to her feet and grabbing her purse.

"Charvette, wait," Kinston called behind her, quickly digging into his pocket to pull out enough cash to cover their meals and a generous tip.

"Wait for what, Kinston? I don't date married men and you're still married." She forced a smile on her face. "You were honest and up front instead of pretending to be single, and I appreciate that. Dinner was great and I've enjoyed your company, but it ends here." Charvette glanced at her watch and sighed. "I can't believe I wasted my whole evening with someone who has no potential," she said under her breath.

"Let me at least get you a room for the night. It's too late for you to get on the road to head to New York."

"No thank you."

"Charvette, please. I'm not asking to sleep with you. You can have the room to yourself. It's not even about that. I would just really like to get to know you better. I know my situation is not ideal, but it is what it is." He paused while she looked at him in silence, contemplating his offer.

It's too late to be driving, and if he's gonna pay for it, why not? she reasoned.

"We can do breakfast in the morning, maybe win a few dollars, and you can be on your way to your shopping trip," he persuaded. "Now, if I had a wife at home, I would not be stupid enough to spend the night at a hotel and not go home at all."

"It is kinda late to be driving," Charvette replied, revealing her weakening stance. "All right, but don't come knocking on my room door tonight."

"Of course not," Kinston answered, with a smile. "You won't hear from me all night long."

Kinston kept his word, although secretly Charvette wished he would have at least attempted to visit her room, just to give her ego a boost. The next morning after a pleasant breakfast and a few rounds with the slot machines, they both were headed to New York in separate vehicles.

By the time Charvette made it back to Virginia, she was convinced that there was no way Kinston could be in an active marital relationship. He had spent the entire week with her in New York, wining, dining, and spending money on her. Even though she'd come home with more bags than she could barely fit into her trunk, she had pulled out her wallet only two or three times the entire week.

Now, as she sat waiting for his arrival, she was frustrated with herself for letting their six-month relationship evolve the way it had. Three months earlier, Kinston shared that Naomi had shown up on his doorstep out of the blue with what she called a revelation from God on how to save her marriage and restake her claim on her husband.

Putting his cell phone on speaker, he played a message left by Naomi.

"Kinston, I am not gonna sit back and let the devil take from me what God has blessed me with. You are *my* man! God gave you to *me,* and I'm gonna do whatever it takes to get my marriage back," she spoke in a wobbly voice punctuated by a few tearful gasps. "I'm gonna pray for us right now, hallelujah, 'cause I know what God has for me is for me!" Naomi continued in a string of charismatic unknown tongues peppered with a few more hallelujahs. "I count it done!" she yelled. "I count it done!"

Kinston ended the call and shrugged. "She's crazy," he commented, clipping the phone back on his hip, then wrapping his arms around Charvette. "I'm with my baby now. It ain't nothing she can do to take me away from you." He planted kisses on her face and neck as he led her backward to her bedroom and made love to her all night long.

That seemed like forever ago. While he claimed to be ignoring his wife's pleas for reconciliation, Charvette noticed that he had become less and less accessible to her.

Having drifted off to sleep, Charvette was awakened twenty minutes later by Kinston's tapping on the door. Immediately she jumped to her feet, smoothed her dress down, and patted her hair before grabbing a peppermint from a candy dish on the table and slipping it between her teeth. Mixed emotions consumed her as she opened the door and looked at the man she was in love with. She'd been anxious and excited about seeing him, which caused a half smile, yet he was two hours late, which contributed to her half frown. Confusion about why he hadn't called fought for its own space in her mind, while love oozed its way between the other three emotions. Impeccably dressed in a black Valentino suit, with a light blue shirt and coordinating tie and a pair of Prada loafers covering his feet, Kinston wrapped his arms around Charvette and whispered, "I'm so sorry I'm late," which further softened her anger. "I couldn't get out of the lab, and you know we can't take our phones in there with us. I got here as quickly as I could."

"You sure it wasn't Naomi dragging you off to Bible study and then for a little private church," she teased, knowing Kinston worked long hours. The more kisses he landed on her warm flesh, the more she opened to him until they both melted into the cushions of her couch in a heated sexual frenzy.

Minutes later after they'd both found satisfaction, Kinston heaved himself to his feet and began straightening his clothes. "I can't stay, babe. I have to be back in the lab first thing in the morning." He slid his feet back into his loafers, then bent down to kiss Charvette on the cheek.

"Well, what about dinner? I didn't eat waiting for you to get here," she griped.

"I know, babe, but it can't be helped. Until we get this new product through final testing, it's just hard for me to plan anything. I'll be glad to run out and get you something so you don't have to go to bed hungry," he offered. "You want some Mc-Donald's or something?"

Charvette chewed on the inside of her lip, feeling cheap and used. "McDonald's?"

"Well, whatever you want, babe," he said nonchalantly. "There's a Chick-fil-A not too far from here. Do you want that instead?"

Charvette stared at him incredulously, unable to find an appropriate response that didn't include curse words. "You know what? Don't worry about it. I'll be all right." She tugged at the banded portion of her dress that circled her upper thighs.

"You sure?" he asked, giving no attention to her sudden attitude. Charvette gave no response but tried to stare a hole in Kinston's head instead. "Well?"

"I don't want anything," she said as a single tear of anger, frustration, and pain seeped from her right eye.

"I'll call you when I get home," he ended. After kissing her cheek once more, he exited, hopped into his Sebring, and pulled off.

I'm Just Asking

Seated behind a desk with monitoring head-phones over her ears, Micah finished entering pay-roll hours for one of her sales teams as she listened to an employee place an outbound call. Although Micah maintained a professional demeanor, she fumed at the fact that instead of Anthony McDon-ald being in his cubicle managing his team, he had not yet shown up for work, leaving her to pick up his load, rather than focus on her duties as a man-ager. To top it off, his payroll entry was a day late, as she'd been notified by an e-mail from the HR department that morning, which put employees at risk of not being paid on time.

"Good morning. May I speak to Sarah Teebly please?"

"This is Sarah. Are you selling something?"

"No, ma'am, I'm not selling anything. I just wanted to let you know about the great long-distance rates you can now get on your home phone. You do still make long-distance calls, right?"

"Umm, yeah, but I make them from my cell, so I wouldn't be interested."

"I understand that, ma'am, but what kind of service do you have on your home phone?"

"No, really, I'm good thanks."

"Well, ma'am, just let me ask you this one question. If something . . ."

"Listen, I'm not interested and I'm hanging up now." Instantly the clamor of the phone being slammed down resonated in the sales rep's ear.

"You need to make sure you are stating your first and last name in the opening of the call, Lenise," Micah coached from her seat.

"I did say my first and last name," Lenise argued.

"No, you didn't. Stop letting the customers throw you off track." Micah struck her keyboard a few times to update the team's sales performance. "You need to get three more sales before lunchtime, and you're not going to be able to do it if you don't stay focused," she added, lifting herself from her seat and walking off. *And I have a wedding to pay for and need every bit of productivity I can get,* Micah thought.

Her career at TeleDynamics had been pretty rewarding over the past four years. She'd started there as a telemarketing rep during her senior year of college and had fully taken advantage of the company's management development training and promotional opportunities. She now managed a team of five supervisors, Anthony being one of them, who each had twenty or so sales reps reporting to them. While the pay afforded her a few of life's luxuries, most days she felt like she was in an adult day-care center with a bunch of grown babies.

She took a quick walk through the sales floor, where the rest of her team sat; stopped by the break room to pick up a bacon, egg, and cheese croissant and a bottle of water; then strolled to her own desk, already formulating the words she would use for Anthony's write-up.

"Micah, how's it going today?" David Ingram ran his fingers through his spiked haircut.

"Pretty well, thank you. My teams are off to a solid start this morning," she responded, with a smile to her boss.

"Great. What's your focus today?"

"I'm hosting a few monitoring sessions with Suzanne from quality to make sure we're calibrated. Why don't you sit in with us?"

"I'm not sure if I'll have time today. I'm still trying to pull some stats together for the executive review tomorrow." He pushed his metro framed lenses up on his nose. "As a matter of fact, would you mind sharing your thoughts on why there's been a decrease in performance for our weekend shift?"

"Don't you think your weekend shift manager would be better able to speak on that, David?" Here he was again trying to pile more on her plate to free up some golf time for himself.

"He's just not as polished with his presentation skills as I'd like him to be. You can actually get all the information you need from him, but I'd like you to do the actual presentation."

"Let me try to get with Steven and see what I can pull together," Micah responded, being careful not to commit.

"The reporting team will probably be able to give you some numbers to work with as well," he suggested, trying to rope her in more tightly to his request.

"I'll follow up with you sometime this afternoon and let you know how things stand."

"Great. Thanks, Micah." David's long-legged strides moved him quickly out of range to overhear Micah mock him.

"Great. Thanks, Micah," she repeated in a whine as she crinkled her nose.

Before she reached her desk, Anthony whizzed by her carrying four bags filled with Styrofoam boxes.

"Good morning," he blurted. "Sorry I missed this morning's meeting. I promised my team breakfast this morning."

"Come see me at my desk before you leave for the day," Micah responded, not stopping her movement.

"Whatever," Anthony mumbled, certain that he was out of Micah's hearing range.

Anthony had no intention of circling back around to Micah's desk, hoping he could inconspicuously leave the building and start his weekend. Then with him being on vacation all next week, by the time he came back to work, Micah would have long forgotten what she wanted to meet with him about.

He'd managed to avoid her entirely as the day uneventfully dragged by. Knowing Micah's general routine, he predicted that by the time he released his team at the end of their shift, he'd have a small window of opportunity to jet out the back door before Micah's management development training session would be over. He had started packing his briefcase right at 3:15 to prepare for the 3:30 shift change. Standing up at his desk, he peered over the sectioned cubicle partitions on the sales floor toward the managers' area, which was a cluster of desks positioned behind a glass wall, with each desk area separated by partitions on each side. Micah's suit jacket was draped over the back of her chair and an array of papers lay scattered on her desk. Looking around, he pulled out his cell phone and maneuvered his thumb over the number pad to send a text message.

> See you in a few—you know how I like my
> sugar, so have it ready.

He refreshed his stats screen once more, then shook his head, disappointed that his team had not converted enough residential phone lines to meet its daily goal. "Pshh, forget it," he dismissed before logging out of the system and heading for the door. He was stopped dead in his tracks as he rounded the bend toward the Management Only exit and found Micah standing there, as if she'd been patiently waiting on him.

"Glad I caught you before you left. Come on over to my desk. There are a few things we need to discuss."

"Well, I kinda had something to do this evening and I'll be late if I don't head out now."

"I understand, but let me first say, while your team gets off at three-thirty, your shift doesn't end until five o'clock, so why you're trying to tip out the back door at"—she paused momentarily to glance at her wrist, then continued—"three-thirty-five is a little bit of a mystery to me." Then, leaving no room for rebuttal, she added, "But I tell you what, why don't you explain that while we walk to my desk." Anthony mumbled a choice word under his breath. "I'm sorry; I didn't hear you." Her raised brows suggested that he repeat his obscenity loud enough for her to hear.

"I ain't say nothing," he huffed. His frustration was expressed in his fast and heavy footsteps. "How long is this gonna take, 'cause I do have something to do."

"I'll let you determine that," she replied as she reached for her access badge, hanging from a pull cord on her hip. After she quickly swiped it through the card reader, the door released and she pushed through, then held the door open for Anthony to pass by her. He walked to her desk and plopped in a seat, letting his messenger bag fall to the floor.

"So what?" he asked, coaxing her to get on with whatever she had planned to do. He picked up a hand puzzle and began toying with it. "If you gone write me up, go 'head. I got somewhere to be."

Keeping her composure, Micah inhaled deeply before beginning her next sentence. "First, I want to talk about your performance."

"What about it?" He shrugged, pretending to be consumed in thought with the toy he held.

"Why don't you tell me what's going on with it." With raised brows, Micah sat back slightly in her chair and laced her fingers together. Anthony hadn't made his sales goal in three months, despite Micah's coaching efforts and leadership.

"This crap y'all giving us to call ain't worth a damn," he answered. "I mean, if y'all want somebody to produce some numbers, we need some good data," he complained. "Almost every household the dialer calls is a wrong number, or the person has been called ten times already."

"So what you are telling me is that, as a supervisor, you are doing everything you can to properly manage your data, your processes, your team, and your business?" she questioned.

"Yup," he said without thought or feeling.

"So the fact that your team is not at staffing head count doesn't play a factor in your inability to reach your numbers?" As she spoke, Micah flipped over a sheet of paper that listed the names of the employees who reported to Anthony. He was understaffed by six heads and had no recruit attempts or completed interviews. "You're only at sixty-two percent of headcount," she pointed out.

"I don't have time to interview. That's HR's job." He dismissed the notion with a wave of his hand.

"What about you reporting to work late? Do you think that has anything to do with it?"

"I called in, didn't I?" Anthony ranted for another three minutes, making excuses for his substandard work performance.

Realizing that Anthony was not going to take accountability for his actions, Micah cut to the chase. She revealed another document that read "Written Warning" across the top. "The bottom line is this is a sales job, and you are a sales supervisor, and right now, you aren't meeting expectation. When we talked last month, there were a few key actions that you were to execute, one of which was to get your team's headcount up to one hundred percent. Not only have you failed to do that, but you are showing an alarming trend of frequent absences and late arrivals." After a gap of silence, she continued, "I'll need your signature on this document."

"Whatever, man," he uttered, practically snatching the paper from Micah's hand and scribbling his signature across the bottom. "By the way, I need to be off on Friday so I'll be taking a vacation day."

"Excuse me?" Micah asked dubiously, as Friday was only two days away.

"I said I'ma be on vacation on Friday." Anthony pushed the paper toward her and got to his feet.

"Did you submit a vacation request?"

"I'm submitting it now."

"Vacation requests are to be submitted two weeks prior. I know you know that."

"Something came up and I just found out about it," he said flatly as he smoothed his mustache with his thumb and forefinger.

"I can't approve the request, Anthony."

"Well, I'll take a personal day then."

She pulled an employee attendance calendar out of his file, which reflected several red X's indicating days he had not reported to work, then responded, "You don't have anymore personal days."

"I'll just call in sick then." Anthony pulled his phone from the clip on his side and began sending another text message.

"You'll just call in sick?" Micah tapped her pen on the desktop, unable to believe Anthony's audacity.

"I already told you I need to be off. I tried to be straight with you and take a vacation day, but you don't wanna give it to me, so I'll call in sick."

"Sick time is to be used for incidental illnesses, not in place of vacation, so if you call in sick, I'll need you to bring me a doctor's note. Have a good evening," Micah replied with finality before picking up her ringing phone. "This is Micah," she spoke into the mouthpiece as she turned her attention to the phone call.

Anthony cursed under his breath, calling Micah out of her name.

"Excuse me?"

"I ain't say nothing," Anthony mumbled as he started to exit. *But I got something for your ass.* "I'ma go talk to HR 'cause I don't think it's fair that you wrote me up and you ain't even gave me the stuff I supposed to have to do my job right in the first place."

"Help yourself, Anthony," she said confidently, knowing that her disciplinary actions were justified.

"Ms. Abraham, are you there?" a consultant called out, bringing Micah's focus back to the phone.

"Yes, I am. How can I help you?" she said, rolling her eyes at Anthony's turned back.

"This is Stacie from Exquisite Bridal Boutique. I was calling to let you know that your headpiece did come in today and you can pick it up whenever you're ready."

"Great! That's perfect timing, since I wanted to try some new hairstyles this weekend. What time does your shop close this evening?"

"We'll be here until six."

Micah frowned as she glanced at her watch. She still had to pull the presentation data together for David as well as fully document the conversation she'd just had with Anthony and get some advice from the human resources staff. "I don't think I'll make it by there this evening, but I'll be in sometime tomorrow to pick it up," she ended. She then dialed Jules Turnberry's extension.

"Jules speaking," the HR generalist answered.

"Hey, Jules, got a question for you. Did Anthony McDonald happen to stop by your office?"

"He did. As a matter of fact, he just left."

Micah sighed loudly. "Well, I guess it's my turn to come visit. I'll need your take on what to do with him. You got a few minutes?" she spoke as she gathered Anthony's file in her hand.

"Sure, come on by," he offered.

Micah went to Jules's office, and within ten minutes, she had explained her challenges with Anthony, then asked Jules for his recommendation on how to best handle the situation.

"Here's the thing," he started, pushing a pair of glasses up the bridge of his nose. "If he calls in sick, there is really nothing you can do about it, even if it is premeditated, so to speak. Now I have to ask you this: do you require all of your employees to bring in doctor's notes when they call in sick?"

Right away, Micah knew where Jules was headed. "No, unless they are out for three or more days."

"So you know you won't be able to put him on any kind of disciplinary action if he comes in without a note, right? It's important to be fair and consistent with all of your employees; you can't require from one if you don't require from all," he finished, leaning back and placing his hands behind his head.

"You're pretty much saying there's nothing I can do."

"I'm afraid not. Just make sure you document everything."

Micah blew out a puff of air as she rose to her feet. "All right, well thanks. I'll keep you posted on how things develop."

"And I'll be here to support you." Jules stood

to escort Micah to his office door. "How are your wedding plans coming along?"

"Wonderfully, but I never realized how much work planning a wedding could be," she replied.

"Well, the groom is definitely a lucky man."

Micah blushed. "Thanks, Jules."

Double O Sevenette

Erin pulled into the parking lot of Gideon's apartment complex without having to be buzzed in at the gate. She shook her head, thinking about the extra money he paid in rent for an amenity that was more often malfunctioning than operating properly.

The lot was unusually full, causing Erin to have to park farther down from Gideon's door than she'd like. She passed his black Acura, positioned in its assigned space, then drove several yards away to an empty slot designated for visitors. She lifted the Scrabble game from her passenger's seat as she dialed Gideon's number so he could open his door for her. Much to her surprise, Gideon didn't answer. She dialed again, thinking that maybe he'd just been in the bathroom, but again there was no answer. Able to view Gideon's windows from where she sat, she was certain he was home as not only did his car sit outside his door but lights were on in his living room and Gideon was a stickler about turning off lights upon leaving a room.

"What the . . ." she uttered as she dialed his number once more. Rather than get out of her vehicle, she sat in place staring at Gideon's door and windows, anger rising within her. She quickly dialed Micah's number but hung up as soon as the call transferred over to voice mail. Next she pushed in the digits that would connect her to Victori, who answered after only two rings.

"You busy?" Erin asked.

"Just sitting here painting my toenails, why? What's up?"

"Girl, I'm out here at Gideon's house. We are supposed to play Scrabble tonight, right?"

"Okay." Victori layered a second coat of electric blue polish on her big toe, then blew gently.

"Why is his car parked right outside his door, but he's not answering his phone?"

"I don't know. Maybe his phone is on vibrate or something."

"His house phone? I don't think so. Something is going on and I'm about to find out what."

"Didn't you have to call him to get in the gate?"

"No, it was wide open, as usual, so I just drove on in. He's in there because his lights are on. He knew I was coming, and I'm only about ten minutes early, so why is he not answering the phone?"

"Go to the door and see who he got up in there."

"I think I'm going to sit out here and watch for a minute," Erin said, leaning back in her seat and setting her eyes on Gideon's front door. "I'm going to be Double O Sevenette tonight. I don't care if I have to spend the night in my car."

"You want me to come out there with you?" Victori offered.

"No, I'm good, but stay by the phone just in case I need some backup!" Although the two giggled as they ended the call, Erin was seething. She switched on her car stereo just as the DJ introduced Beyonce's "Ring the Alarm." Micah wasn't very familiar with the lyrics but knew a song about a woman's fury when she heard it, and sang the few lines she knew.

In the fifteen minutes that she sat observing from her vehicle, Gideon's bedroom light came on, then was turned off momentarily, then was switched on and off again. Erin gasped out loud when Gideon's door finally eased open and out stepped a tall pecan-complexioned woman with her hair cut closely to her scalp and tapered at the sides and neck, with Gideon trailing a half step behind. Gideon's eyes scanned the parking lot, taking note of the visitor's vehicles in the spaces closest to his home, but not looking farther down the sidewalk where Erin was positioned. He cupped the woman's rounded behind, encased in a pair of tight jeans, and planted a kiss on her lips. Erin sat motionless with her mouth gaped open but then quickly zoomed in on the couple with her iPhone and captured a photo for the record. After pecking her twice more, he walked the woman to a white Hyundai Santa Fe, opened her door, and kissed her again once she was seated inside.

Glancing down at his wrist, Gideon checked the time, then took a seat in his own car. No sooner than he'd started the ignition, he dialed Erin's number. She answered calmly, as if she had not just witnessed him exchanging saliva with another woman.

"Hey, beautiful," he cooed. "Where are you? I thought you were coming over." Slowly he backed his vehicle out of his parking space and pulled out of the lot. Erin followed closely behind, unnoticed due to the brightness of her headlights.

"I'm on my way," she lied. "I would have been there earlier but I accidentally left the Scrabble game at the house and had to go back to get it. I tried to call you but your cell went straight to voice mail and you didn't answer your home phone. You're at home?" she continued.

"I'm on my way there now," he answered, making a right at the intersection. "I had to run out and pick up a few things from Wal-Mart. I got in there and started looking at those two-for-ten dollar DVDs and lost track of time."

"Oh, well good thing I wasn't on time," Erin replied as she watched him make a U-turn and head back toward his apartment. "Did you find anything good?"

"Nah, they didn't have anything I was interested in buying."

"Really? All those movies and you couldn't find anything, huh?"

"I was hoping they would have something for us to cuddle up to tonight." He whipped his car back in its parking space. "So where are you?"

"Umm, I'm about five minutes away," she answered, cruising back into the gate convinced the distance between them made by the cars that intervened at the U-turn would allow him time enough to enter his home and not see her driving up.

"Hurry up, babe. I can't wait to see you."

"I can't wait to see you either." Erin bit into her lower lip to keep from adding on a couple more choice words. She ended the call with Gideon, then called Victori back. "I hope you got some cash just in case I get locked up tonight."

"Don't do nothing stupid," Victori warned. "'Cause this ain't a pay week, and you'll be in there for a minute."

Erin giggled despite her bitterness toward Gideon. She quickly filled her friend in on what had taken place over the last twenty-five minutes. "All right I'll call you back. Either me or the cops. Bye, girl," she smirked as she opened her car door, left the game in the car, stepped out onto the asphalt, and smoothed her halter dress with her hands. Erin stepped purposefully to Gideon's door. Before she finished knocking, Gideon opened the door and attempted to embrace her, but he immediately sensed her lack of reciprocation.

"What's wrong, babe," he asked, with a crinkled brow. "You're not excited to see me?" He tried wrapping his arms around her a second time, but she pushed past him.

"Let me at least get in the house." With her back to him she rolled her eyes and plopped down on the couch.

"What's wrong with you?" he exclaimed a second time, closing the door, then taking a seat beside her. "Where's the Scrabble game?"

"So you couldn't find a movie, huh?" Erin twisted her lips as she stared blankly at the television displaying an encore presentation of *Hell's Kitchen*.

"Why do you keep asking me that, Erin? I told you they didn't have anything."

"They didn't have anything, or you didn't get a chance to look good?"

"I could have stayed in there longer, but I was rushing to get back here to you once I realized what time it was."

Maintaining her composure, Erin now wanted

to see how far Gideon would carry his lie. "Well, I'm glad you came home in a flash just for me."

"I can do something else for you too, baby," he said, lifting a hand to fondle one of Erin's breasts, but she slapped his hand away and looked him directly in his eyes with her brows raised and a half smile.

"Baby," she said with a hint of excitement, "I finally figured it out about those panties I found under my bed."

"There was never anything to figure out. I told you I bought those for you when we went to D.C. that time. I don't know how you could have forgotten that." He shrugged, then lay across the couch to rest his head in her lap and began fumbling with the television remote.

"Right, right," Erin chanted in response. "And here I was thinking that they belonged to some tall, big-bootied bald-headed woman."

"Who?" Gideon kept his response nonchalant overcast by a clueless tone, not turning away from the TV.

"You know," she chuckled, circling her fingers through his wavy hair and against his scalp. "Some wench whom you're seeing behind my back."

"Who in the world are you talking about, baby?" he said, feigning ignorance. "Why would I waste my time with someone else when I have you?" he dismissed.

Erin's blood heated to a slow boil. "How is it that you can lie here in my lap and so comfortably lie to me, Gideon?"

Right away he detected the change in her voice tone and struggled to gain control of the situation. He turned his head away from the TV and looked up at her face. "Look," he started, attempting to convey assertiveness, "I haven't seen you all week long because of your job working you like a slave. I have been looking forward to seeing you all day long, and I really don't want to waste this time arguing over some nonsense." Erin bit her tongue as she looked down at Gideon's face, barely able to stand the sight of him. "Now, you had a chip on your shoulder when you came in here, and I don't know what that was all about, but you need to calm down."

"Get off me, Gideon," she spoke evenly.

"What? For what? No," he refused.

"I'm ready to go home."

"No," he countered, nestling against her stomach. "I wanted to see you—you're here, and you ain't going nowhere." He began to run his hand up and down her left shin and calf.

Though infuriated, Erin sat ten more minutes pretending to focus on the aspiring restaurateurs who were being called out of their names by world-class chef Gordon Ramsay, but in her mind, she could only think about what she'd witnessed earlier and how badly she wanted to spit in Gideon's face.

His ringing phone pulled him away from her lap, and he trodded toward the kitchen to answer. Erin sat attentively listening to his conversation.

"Hey," he started after glancing at the Caller ID display. "You home already?" Right away Erin knew it was Triple B: big-bootied baldie. Gideon always told Erin to call him once she'd reached home, and obviously he did the same for everyone. He padded down the hallway to the bathroom, covering the remainder of his conversation. Erin had thought to tiptoe to the bathroom door to eavesdrop but knew she'd seen and heard enough. Instead, she used the opportunity to let herself out, fighting back tears on the way to her car.

"Why can't I find the right one?" she questioned as she thought back to every man who'd ever been a part of her life romantically. They all had been cheaters, abusers, druggies, or in some other way unfit. Tearing out of Gideon's lot, she thought to switch her phone off, knowing he'd be calling in the next few seconds. *Maybe I should just let go of men altogether and cross over to women,* she thought for a split second but was instantly repulsed. "Nah!"

Before her hand could locate the phone in the bottom of her purse, it began to ring. Pulling it out seconds later, she rolled her eyes but answered anyway.

"Why did you leave like that?" Gideon began.

"I just had to go," she responded nonchalantly.

"But why, baby? You had just got here."

"My period is on and I didn't have any tampons or pads there," she lied. "I kept trying to tell you I needed to leave."

"Oh," Gideon replied in acceptance. "You could have just said that, though."

"I know how stupid you act whenever I mention my cycle, so I was trying to keep it on the low."

"Call me next week then," he said, bringing their conversation to an end.

Ready, Set, No!

Rossi wrapped his arms around Micah as tightly as he could, then lifted her petite frame off the floor. "I love you. You know that, right?"

"Oh, boy," she giggled as he nuzzled her neck. "You must have done something you ain't had no business doing." She turned her head toward his and pecked his cheek. "Put me down before I burn up the food. I hope you're hungry."

"Why can't it be that I just want to show my future wife some love? If I only show you love when I've done something wrong, I'm going to have to work on that," Rossi said nervously as he lowered Micah to the floor, stuffed his hands into his pockets, and followed her into the kitchen. "What are you cooking, babe? Whatever it is, it smells good." He tugged on the handle of the oven door and peered inside at the lasagna that was just beginning to brown on top. "Oh, I haven't had good lasagna in a long time," he commented, then licked his lips. "This looks delicious, baby."

"Okay, I know you've done something now. You

never compliment me on my cooking. Is your ex-girlfriend in town or something?" she teased. She believed Rossi to be a faithful man, so his lack of response meant nothing to her. "Grab the salad out of the fridge, please." As Micah pulled two wineglasses down from the overhead rack, she noticed the uncomfortable expression on Rossi's face. "You all right?" she asked, turning to get dinner plates out of the cabinets. Without allowing Rossi any chance to respond, she continued, "You know, I saw the sweetest proposal on TV today. It was on *Everybody Loves Raymond*. Do you watch that show?"

"No."

"Well, Raymond's brother, Robbie, is a cop, right? So he got all his cop friends to pull up all crazy in front of a restaurant while his girlfriend was coming out and kinda scared her. Then they were like 'you have the right to remain single and anything you say can and will be held against you in a church of God, and if you don't have a husband, one will be provided for you.' Then right after that Robbie comes walking around the corner in, like, a lieutenant's uniform or something and gets down on his knee and proposes!" Micah babbled. Pretending to wipe a tear from her eye, she added, "It was so beautiful."

There was a pregnant pause that hung in the air before Rossi responded. "Baby, I need to ask you something."

"Okay?" she questioned with raised brows as she slid insulated mitts onto both hands to lift the pasta dish from the oven. "What is it, baby?"

"Hold on a minute." Rossi reached for his cell phone, glanced at the number, and answered right away. "Hey, Rom," he spoke to his twin, with a smile. "What you know good?"

"Nothing right now," she answered, trying to steady her shaky voice. "I was just calling to see how you were."

"What's wrong? It sounds like you're crying." Rossi moseyed into the living room with the phone glued to his ear.

"I'm all right." Romni cleared her throat. "I just wanted to see if I could come visit soon. I know you're busy with work and everything and you don't have to take off to babysit me. I just want to get away."

Not fooled by Romni's poor attempt at trying to mask her situation, Rossi didn't hesistate to welcome his sister. "You know you can come up here anytime." He paused for a second, then continued, "But what's going on with you?

Romni coughed twice as she lowered herself onto the mattress and box spring on her bedroom floor and stared at her dingy pillowcase. "I um . . ." She shook her head in silence. "I'm just tired of getting beat on, Rossi."

Rossi blew a long stream of air through his puckered lips. He'd had several conversations with his sister in the past about her abusive relationship, but they all were for naught. Romni had always found reason to stay in her mayhem. "I've heard you say that before, Rom," he measured carefully. "And I've tried to help you, but you've got to want it for yourself, baby girl."

"I do want it, Rossi." Her voice cracked as she smudged a trickle of tears with the heel of her hand. "I guess I've just never known how to get there."

"Well, I'll tell you what. If you need to come

here, come on. You can stay as long as you need to," he offered, not actually believing that she would come.

"Can you send me the money to get there? There's a Western Union right—"

"Rom, you know I can't send any money." The seriousness in his voice affirmed that he would not send cash. "I can send you a ticket, but money is out of the question." Rossi glanced over at Micah and held up a single finger, indicating that he'd be just another minute, then winked his eye and blew her a kiss. "When do you want to come?"

"In the next couple of days if it's not going to cost you too much."

"Well I'ma tell you like this—a dollar is gonna be too much if you don't put your behind on that plane." Romni didn't comment. "Don't make me waste my money, Romni."

"I'm not," she whined in response. "I really wanna come. I'm seriously thinking about moving there and, you know, starting over."

"Is that right?" Rossi asked rhetorically. Before Romni could respond, Rossi hastened a suggestion. "I'll tell you what. I'll go ahead and book you a round-trip flight for the day after tomorrow. I'll be down there for the family reunion in a couple of weeks, so if you're still serious about relocating you can ride back here with me then. How much stuff do you have?"

"Nothing really, just some clothes and stuff." Her eyes quickly scanned the room, her gaze landing on three large piles of dirty laundry, a collection of beer bottles, and a dented soda can holding a few sticks of incense.

"Do you mean it this time, Rom?" Rossi asked sincerely.

Romni pressed her lips together, apprehensive about her answer, knowing that she still hadn't made a solid decision. Nonetheless, she murmured a response: "Yeah, I am." She suddenly jumped to her feet, hearing T-Dog's voice through her open bedroom window. "I gotta go, big brother," she rushed as she slid a finger through the slats in her miniblinds and peeked out. "I love you," she blurted, then ended the call.

"I love . . ." Rossi glanced down at the screen of his cell after realizing his sister had hung up. "You too," he finished, then rejoined Micah in the kitchen.

"How's your sister?" Micah generically asked.

"She's all right. She's coming to visit in a couple of days."

"Great!" Micah beamed. "I look forward to meeting her, seeing how I never had a sister." Though Micah and Rossi had been involved for a year and a half, she'd yet to meet his mother and sister. "And it would be great to meet at least one of your family members before the wedding," she said sarcastically.

She'd been after Rossi about taking her home to meet his mom since he'd proposed to her five months ago. After a euphoric session of lovemaking that had completely blown his mind, leaving him confused even about his very name, they both sat in a jetted tub, surrounded by fragrant bubbles and lit candles, with an aura of love, lust, and passion hanging in the air. Rossi was simply beside himself as he wrapped his arms around her shoulders and smoothed tendrils of her wet hair away from her face. For him, the moment couldn't have been more perfect, as he heard no other sound than her relaxed breathing as she leaned back into his chest. So the words came easily.

"I love you, Micah," he whispered in her ear before blowing a few bubbles from her shoulder. "And I hope you take seriously what I'm about to say." He kissed her cheek and lifted her left hand from the water, then circled her ring finger with his thumb and index finger. "I know this is not the way this usually goes, since I don't have a ring in my hand, but . . . will you be my wife?" Micah whipped her head around to look into Rossi's eyes. He leaned forward slightly to meet her lips, planting soft kisses against her warm flesh. "This time next year," he said between kisses, "will you marry me, Micah?"

She studied his face for only a second before responding. "Yes baby!" she said excitedly, pressing her lips more aggressively against his. "Yes!"

He caressed her tenderly with his hands and lips, stoking the fire that had been on slow burn until it became fully inflamed. For the next two hours, they made love body, mind, and soul, with him whispering the request "be my wife" over and over again.

Not even a week had passed before Rossi came to his senses about his sexually provoked proposal, but once he did, he could have kicked himself. It wasn't that he didn't love Micah; he just didn't love her enough to truly commit and simply had not found the right moment to renege. At the same time, he wasn't quite ready to let go of her. He knew that going back on his proposal would be the kiss of death for their relationship, so he did what he thought best—he held on as best he could and simply tried to avoid any marriage and wedding-related circumstances like the plague.

The times he found himself forced into a situation, he merely played along, like the few times she dragged him to the jewelry counter as they shopped in the mall. As he had slid ring after ring on her finger, he had pretended to be dissatisfied with what the stores offered.

"That's just not the one I want you to have, baby," he'd said. "This hardly symbolizes the love I have for you," he'd said. "This looks like a starter ring, not a ring for my queen," he'd said. Micah had fallen for it every time, but he knew his excuses were becoming less tolerable. So tonight, he'd decided to bite the bullet and buy himself more time.

"Anyway, what'd you have to ask me?"

Rossi stood in front of the salad bowl on the counter and pretended to take interest in retossing its contents. He scooped and forked the mixture of fresh greens, cherry tomatoes, sliced cucumbers, and chopped walnuts as he struggled to find his next words. "Well . . . I've been thinking about . . . a few things, you know," he stammered. "And, uh . . . it's hard for me to say this . . . but uh . . . would you mind if we pushed the wedding date back a little bit?" After a few seconds of silence, Rossi found the courage to look Micah in the eye. She stared incredulously at him, waiting for some type of explanation, but Rossi remained silent for nearly a minute.

"Yes, I would mind," Micah answered stoically. A firm hand placed on her hip and her furrowed brows were the only expressions of her rising anger as she was careful not to raise her voice.

"But you haven't even heard my reasons."

"Jimmy crack corn and I don't care about your reasons. I said I mind," she repeated, this time her voice rising an octave. "But why don't you go ahead and share with me why you feel it necessary to push the date back." Using a spatula, Micah dug into the hot casserole dish and slammed a dollop of lasagna onto a plate for her fiancé, then stabbed the center with a fork before shoving it at him. Rossi took the plate from her hands, added a portion of salad, then took a seat at her Bistro Pub dining table, swiveling in his bar stool trying to find a little comfort. "I'm listening," she said calmly, although rage was festering within her.

"I'll wait until you sit down."

Micah took her time placing her own food carefully on her plate, eased it onto the table, then poured two glasses of wine before taking her seat across from Rossi. She quickly whispered her grace, then began eating silently, waiting for Rossi to present his case.

"Just hear me out, baby." He reached across the table for Micah's free hand, but she drew back and placed it in her lap.

"Micah, don't act like that," he said, almost pleading.

"Talk," she ordered. Rossi inhaled and pushed a long slow breath from his puckered lips as he looked at the floor. "Get on with it, Rossi!" she barked, becoming more and more irritated with his very presence.

"Micah, you know I love you," he began. "You know that. You are the most beautiful and intriguing woman I've ever met, and I do want to marry you." He paused for a few seconds, searching her eyes for a hint of acceptance of his opening lines. Finding none, he continued, "I know that you've made some preparations, but I just need a little more time to make sure that when I marry you I can be the husband you need me to be."

"What the hell does that mean?" Micah garnered a bit of control from somewhere and had returned to her nonchalant voice.

Rossi quickly recalled his rehearsed pitch. "Well, for one, I know you want to start a family right away, and I want to give you that, but I can't say that I'm quite ready for a baby right now. I'm in the midst of my career going to the next level, and I know it's going to require some long hours and extreme sacrifices where work is concerned, and I don't want to cheat you, or my baby, of the time and attention that you both deserve."

"Really?" Micah asked rhetorically, then forked more food into her mouth and sipped from her wineglass.

"I mean, wouldn't you want me home at a reasonable hour every night as your husband? To hold you and make love to you, massage your feet and rub your back? Wouldn't you want me to be able to assist you with raising the kids instead of you being stuck in the house feeling like a single parent?"

Silently fuming, Micah stared up at the ceiling as more words tumbled from Rossi's lips, but she barely heard them. Her gaze floated across the room and rested on a row of books aligned on a shelf. Ironically, she zeroed in on D. V. Bernard's *How to Kill Your Boyfriend (in Ten Easy Steps)*. She had yet to read the book but promised herself she would start on it as soon as Rossi left for the evening. Her own personal how-to list began to form in her mind while Rossi mumbled on in the background.

"Are you even listening to me?" he asked, dropping his fork on his plate. Micah shrugged her shoulders in response, having long disengaged herself from what was being said. He crinkled his brows in frustration, but then straightened them just as quickly and began eating again.

Nothing was heard for ten minutes other than the sound of their forks making contact with their plates. Rossi dared to break the silence. "What are you thinking about, baby?"

"Well, Rossi, to be honest with you, I'm thinking about changing my name to Ludacris because I feel like slapping somebody today," she answered curtly while batting her eyes in rapid succession. "Namely you. Are you finished eating?" Before Rossi could answer, she stood and snatched his plate away, scraped the remainder of his meal in the trash can, and tossed the plate into the sink. She then stepped toward him, snatched the fork from his hand, and threw it in the sink as well. "I suggest you leave now."

Rossi twisted his lips and sat motionless for a few seconds before standing and heading toward the door with measured steps. "I do love you, Micah," he attempted, looking her way with pleading eyes. Micah didn't bother to look up.

"Good night."

Rossi turned the knob, let himself out, and quietly pulled the door closed. Exhaling as if he'd been holding his breath all night, he smiled and spoke out loud to himself, "That didn't go too bad at all."

Micah massaged her temples trying to ease away an oncoming headache while she soaked in a tub of sudsy hot water. The scent of lavender and chamomile just wasn't enough to erase the tension, not to mention the heartache, that Rossi's words had brought on. *Why would he do this? Why is he pulling back?* she questioned in her mind. Against her will, tears slid down her face and merged with the water that covered her breasts. Not caring if her hair got wet, she sank deeper into the bubbles. Contemplating for the next sixty minutes, Micah could come to no conclusion as to why Rossi wanted to change the date of the wedding.

She felt like a pure fool, having made plans for a wedding without even having a ring on her finger, going solely on Rossi's word that he wanted to marry her on January 31, which was just seven months away. She'd trusted that the ring was on its way, but now she really had no reason to believe it. Her eyelids wanted to close in rest, but every time she allowed them to, she saw dollar signs floating in the darkness, reminding her of the money she'd wasted on contract down payments, dated favors, programs, and other wedding paraphernalia.

Micah, you know I love you. You know that. You are the most beautiful and intriguing woman I've ever met, and I do want to marry you. His words played over and over again in her mind as she mentally scanned them for any semblance of truth.

The water had long grown cold before Micah lifted herself from the tub and patted dry. As much as she wanted to believe him, in the deepest and most true chamber of her heart, she felt their relationship dying.

The ringing telephone jarred her from her thoughts. Glancing at the Caller ID, she recognized the number as coming from Charvette's hair salon. Although she didn't feel much like conversing, she answered anyway.

"Hey, Char," she spoke in an exhale.

"Hey. You got a minute?"

"Sure." *Misery loves company, they say,* she thought.

"I think Kinston is back with his wife."

"That's good. Now you have good reason to leave him alone with his married self," Micah replied, taking a seat at her vanity and applying cocoa butter on her face.

"Thanks for your sympathy," Charvette said dryly.

"Charvette, how do you expect me to sympathize when you are seeing a married man? Kinston is someone's husband. What do you want me to say: 'Oh, how could he! That cheating bastard!'? I can't really say that because until he gets a divorce, he's married no matter how rocky he says the marriage is or how crazy he claims his wife to be."

"Okay, but if he is going to get back with her, the least he could do is tell me that up front. I mean, he was up front and honest when we met, so what's stopping him from doing that now?" she replied as she recorded some accounting figures into the computer in her small office. "I guess that's too much like right, though, huh?"

"No, right would have been finalizing his divorce before getting involved with another woman," Micah preached. Silence hung in the air until Micah spoke again. "What makes you think he's been with his wife anyway?"

"He's just been MIA a lot lately, not returning my phone calls, showing up late, or not showing at all."

"Did you ask him if he and his wife were back together?"

"Yes," Charvette whined. "He said they're not

and he's just been working extra hours because they have some new product in the final stages of testing and some bull like that."

"And you don't believe him?"

"I don't know. I want to, but I know Naomi's been calling him and stuff. I mean, we used to be together all the time and all of a sudden he's just acting so different."

"Well you can do one of two things: one, believe him, or two, don't believe him. Either way, until he produces some papers with some signatures on them, he's married and you don't need to be fooling with him in the first place."

"That's easy for you to say, Micah; you got a man. But what about me? When I met Kinston, he wasn't even with that woman."

"So he said."

"He *wasn't!*" Charvette exclaimed.

"How do you know that, Char? Have you been to his house?"

"Yes, and there were no traces of a woman nowhere in that big house he has!"

"Were there traces of him there? How do you know he didn't take you to one of his boys' houses or something? Did you see pictures?"

"Come to think of it, no. Wait—yes I did see . . . oh, no that was something else. No I didn't see any pictures."

"Don't you have pictures up in your house?" Micah questioned.

"Yeah, but guys are different," Charvette answered as she gathered her things to leave the shop for the evening.

"Okay. Well, like I said, you are either going to believe him or not believe him. It's up to you to decide which one you'll do. Now let's talk about me," Micah said, switching gears in an instant. "Rossi came over here and announced that he wants to move the wedding date."

"What? Why?"

"Girl, I don't know. I've been trying to figure that out all evening."

"Well, what did he say?" Charvette questioned as she shut her computer down.

"He basically said he needed more time to get himself together."

"So he has cold feet?" Charvette asked, as a potential reason.

"Who knows. I don't even want to think about it right now. It's making my head hurt," Micah replied, slipping her nude body between her silk sheets. "I'm going to bed." She said her good-byes, then drifted off to sleep only to have wedding day nightmares.

The next morning she opened her front door to find a huge bouquet of beautifully bloomed lavender roses. Instantly a smile crossed her face as she lifted the vase and pulled the small card from its holder.

Micah, all I need is a little time, and I promise I will make you the happiest woman in the world.
                                        Rossi

Sleep, Baby, Sleep

Romni wrapped her arms around her big brother in the tightest embrace her thin arms would allow. "Thank you, Rossi!" She sniffed against his shirt before pulling away. "You just don't know how bad I needed to get out of Georgia."

"You're welcome. I'm glad you're here," Rossi replied, taking Romni's carry-on bag and hoisting it up on his shoulder. "How long are you planning on staying?"

"About a week I guess. Just to try to sort some things out. I just can't think at home, you know?"

"I guess you can't with somebody knocking your brains around every day," he shot, instantly regretting his lack of sensitivity after he saw Romni's smile fade into an expression of hurt, although she said nothing. In a weak attempt to smooth over his harsh words, he draped an arm around her shoulders and pulled her into him as they walked. "You hungry?" She shook her head silently. "Aw, come on, girl, let your big brother take you out to breakfast. You look like you haven't eaten all year with your tiny self."

Romni couldn't help but chuckle; Rossi had always teased her about her size. "I guess I could use some yogurt and a bagel or something."

"Yogurt and a bagel? I'm about to fatten you up like a duck one month before Christmas," he teased. "There's a Waffle House a few blocks up the street, and today you're having waffles with strawberries, sausage with gravy, grits with sugar and butter, toast with jelly, scrambled eggs with cheese, hash browns with onions, and orange juice with pulp."

"You sound like Momma," she said, giggling. "Just because you two have a little belly"—she patted her brother's not-so-flat front—"everybody else is supposed to jump on the bandwagon, huh?"

"Rossi bent his head down to kiss his sister's cheek. "I love you, Romni."

"I love you too," she replied, happier than she'd been in a long time.

Rossi loaded Romni's things into his car and then they got in and headed for the restaurant. "So how is Momma doing?"

"You know Momma; ain't nothing changed. She's complaining about her sugar and her pressure; going to church on Sundays, Wednesdays, and Fridays; and crocheting afghans with those cacklin' women she calls sisters."

Rossi laughed. "You're right—nothing *has* changed, has it?"

"She's mad at you right now because you still haven't told her whether you are coming to the reunion or not."

"I'll give her a call this week," he promised as he reached for his cell phone. Micah's number displayed on the screen. "Hello," he answered.

"Hey, sweetie," Micah chirped.

"How're you doing?" he replied with little enthusiasm.

"I'm fine . . . is everything okay? You sound distracted or something."

"I'm fine. What's up?"

"Nothing," she said, sensing his evasiveness. "I know you said your sister was flying in this morning. Did she get here yet?"

"Yeah, we're headed out to breakfast now," he shared. There was a long pause.

"Oh." Micah felt a twinge of pain that she'd not been invited to join them. Confused that he'd not included her, she struggled to find her next words. "I . . . uh . . . was hoping to meet her. It seems like breakfast this morning would have been a good opportunity since I'll be working the rest of the week." There was an awkward silence as she waited for him to ask her along.

"We'll try to get by there later on," he dismissed. "I'll give you a call when we leave here."

"Okay. Well, have a good time. Love you," she said, trying to mask the sting of his rejection.

"All right, talk to you later." Rossi hung up, intentionally avoiding the exchange of endearment.

"Was that your job or something? You don't have to go, do you?" Romni asked.

"Of course not. My whole day is blocked off to spend with my favorite sister." He smiled as he pushed into her shoulder.

"Your only sister, you mean."

"Yeah, that too. Let's eat," he said, then stopped the car and they both hopped out. "It's just me and you, kid." Once they were seated in a small booth and had placed their breakfast orders, Rossi started digging to discover where Romni's head was. "So let me hear this plan you have."

"It's not actually a plan yet, but I'm definitely going to need some help with whatever I'm tryna do," she said, smoothing her hair back with her hands.

"Which is what?"

"I told you; I'm thinking of moving up here and maybe go to school and make something of myself." She turned her eyes away from Rossi and began to stare blankly out the window. "All I know is I can't keep doing what I'm doing, Rossi," she said, nearing tears. "I'm twenty-eight and all I have to show for it is a pile of excuses." She turned back toward Rossi. "It's time for me to change that."

Their server approached with their meals and set them on the table. "You two let me know if you need anything else. I'll be glad to wait on you," she said, with a smile, before walking off.

"I could probably get a job here," Romni stated. "If I don't know how to do anything else, I know how to bring people a plate of food." She chuckled. "Let's say grace like we used to do when we were kids," she suggested, reaching for Rossi's hands. She closed her eyes and said a brief prayer.

When she opened them again, Rossi was staring at her with a smirk on his face. "I'm glad you're here."

"Thanks, Rossi."

"And I'll help you as long as you want to be helped," he committed.

They continued chatting and laughing over their meal but were interrupted when a tall caramel man dressed in a pair of loose-fitting jeans and a plain white T-shirt approached their table.

"Ay, what's up, man," he said, extending his hand toward Rossi.

"Man, I haven't seen you in a minute!" he

exclaimed as he quickly wiped his hand on a napkin and clasped palms with his friend. "How've you been, Jaison, man?"

"I been aight. You know, making this thang work, that's all." He smiled.

"This is my sister, Romni. Romni, this is Jaison," Rossi introduced. Romni blushed as their hands met for a quick shake.

"Nice to meet you," he said cordially.

"Likewise."

"Well, I ain't gone hold you up, man. I just saw you sitting over here and thought I'd come holla at you. I'm 'bout to get this food and press, man."

"Yeah, man, it was good seeing you," Rossi added as they shook hands a final time. "You still stay out there near Ashton Square?" he asked, referring to the neighborhood where he'd last known Jaison to live.

"Yeah, I ain't gone nowhere; exact same place, man. Guess I've gotten a little comfortable, but I'm probably gonna get a house built or something after I settle down."

"Right, right."

"You still doing the single thing yourself, I see."

"Yeah, man."

"Look, get at me sometimes; let me give you my number," Jaison said. Rossi quickly pulled out his phone and pretended to thumb the digits into the device's memory. As soon as the brother had moved out of hearing range, Romni asked about him.

"What's up with him?"

"Oh, you don't want that. Trust me," Rossi warned. "That's not where your head needs to be right now anyway."

"Okay, okay!" she replied, throwing her hands up. "I was just asking. Calm down; it's not that serious."

"I'm just saying. Don't leave a mess to get into a mess," Rossi said firmly, recalling a few memories of Jaison from college. "That right there ain't nothing you wanna fool with."

"I said okay! So where's the woman in your life? I just knew you'd have somebody on lock by now."

"I mean, I got a couple of friends, but that don't mean much." He shrugged. "And stop being so nosy. You always were trying to stay up in my business." He chuckled as he stabbed at a piece of cut sausage from her plate.

"Whatever! So what else are we gonna do today?" Romni said, switching the subject.

"Whatever you want. I cleared my schedule today to spend with you. I don't know what you had in mind other than probably wanting to relax a little bit."

"Yeah, relaxing sounds right up my alley. But you know what? I should get me a few job applications and fill them out while I'm here. Can I use your address?"

"First things first. How about we start with building the plan?"

"You're right. I'm just excited about the new opportunities ahead of me."

"What about ole boy?" Rossi asked, referring to T-Dog. "Do you think he will try to follow you up here?"

"I don't care what he does, to be honest with you, Rossi. I should have stopped caring the first time he put his hands on me," she said, then lifted her juice to her lips and took a long swallow. "It's time for me to start caring about myself."

"You gonna leave your momma down in Georgia

by herself?" he teased, although he enjoyed seeing a faint glimmer of hope in Romni's eyes.

"Psshhh! Yeah! Momma is a grown woman. She'll be just fine with her gossiping church friends. I need to start living for me!" she exclaimed as she rubbed her now full belly. "And I'll need some new clothes if I eat like this again while I'm here."

The two siblings spent the rest of the day enjoying each other's presence as they made stops around town for Rossi to run errands. By the time the sun set, they'd stopped by Blockbuster's to pick up a few of their childhood favorites, including *The Wiz* and *Brewster's Millions*. In no time, they'd fallen asleep in the den while watching the movies. Romni was enjoying the most restful sleep she'd had in a very long time.

Meanwhile, Micah sat at home hurt and angry that Rossi had never called her back, although she'd called him at least three other times throughout the day.

And back in Georgia, once T-Dog realized Romni wasn't coming home, he decided to keep himself entertained by inviting Crystal, the girl from the apartment above his head, over for the night.

New Opportunities
in New Places

"All management employees please report to the
main conference room for the all hands meeting,"
the receptionist's voice announced through the PA
system, prompting the sales supervisors and managers to end whatever they were working on. Once
everyone was seated in the conference room, David
Ingram opened the meeting in his normal fashion
of thanking his staff for their hard work and contri-
butions, then reviewing the Richmond center's performance against others' in their competing region.

"So all in all we seem to be doing pretty well, but
I'd sure like to take the Glen Allen center down
this month. Can we do it?" He pumped a fist wildly
in the air to motivate his direct reports. He received a response of cheers, applause, and shrill
whistles. "And I'll tell you what I'll do: if we outper-
form Glen Allen, I'll award each supervisor with
five hundred dollars and each manager with one
thousand dollars!" The staff now began to stand

and high-five each other in excitement. "And the top-performing supervisor will get twenty-five hundred dollars, while the top-performing manager will take home five thousand dollars!" Once the motivated employees finished another round of cheering, they all took their seats again.

"I sure could use that money," Micah whispered to Erin. "That would take care of the reception venue, or at least let me pay you a little more for my dress, since I now have more time." Micah smiled, holding on to a mustard seed of faith that there would be a wedding after all.

"Finally, I want to make you all aware that Tele-Dynamics is opening a new site in Charlotte, North Carolina. For those of you seeking upward mobility and promotion within the company, this is an excellent opportunity to go to the next level. They will start their ramp-up process in the next two weeks or so and will need to fill several roles on several levels. If you have individuals on your team who you feel are ready for a management-level position, please share that information with them, and of course I want to encourage anyone who is interested in relocating to talk to your manager. Available positions are posted on our intranet if you'd like to take a look. Now for those of you who have no interest in the relocation part of the ramp, there are sure to be opportunities here at this site as we are able to promote individuals to Charlotte," David shared. "Now let's get out there and take Glen Allen out!" There was a final eruption of cheers before the employees disbursed back to their prospective areas.

Before Micah could reach her desk, three of her supervisors mentioned in passing that they'd be interested in furthering their careers with the Charlotte opportunities. She made a note to set up meeting times with each of them later that afternoon, then logged on to the company's site to research the available positions. In her exploration she found several opportunities that piqued her interest, although she'd never considered relocation. She clicked on a link for a senior relationship manger and began to read the job description but was interrupted by Jules.

"Micah, do you have a few minutes?"

"Sure, Jules." With a quick hand gesture she offered Jules a seat.

"How are things going?"

"Pretty well. What's up?"

Jules sighed before he started again. "I need to talk to you about Anthony McDonald."

"Okay?" Micah questioned.

"He's come to HR quite a few times complaining about your managerial style and stating that you show favoritism. Of course, he doesn't think he is one of your favorites," Jules said jokingly, trying to ease the tension of the situation. "Have you been having more issues with him?"

"Actually, yes. He hasn't made his sales goal in about three months or so, with his performance steadily decreasing, and there have been issues with him not completing payroll on time, causing individuals on his team to not be paid properly, just for starters."

"And you have addressed him regarding these concerns, right?"

"Yes, I have, and of course I have everything properly documented in his file as it should be. Jules, I just don't understand why he is giving me such a fit." Micah slunk backward in her chair and studied the ceiling tiles. "Maybe he will be interested in relocating to Charlotte and getting out of my hair. I don't know how much of him I can take, and he obviously hates me."

"Well, here's what I need to do, Micah. I need to do a random audit on your employee files as part of my responsibility and commitment to look into his complaint," Jules said almost apologetically. "If I can get about three of your files in addition to Mr. McDonald's that will provide me with enough information to move forward."

"No problem at all." Micah reached across her desktop for her keys, unlocked the bottom drawer, and pulled it open. "Here they are at your disposal. Pick any file you'd like," she said, holding her hands up in mock surrender.

"I'm sorry I have to do this, Micah, but I'm already confident that nothing will come of this."

"No apology necessary. I don't mind at all." She rolled backward in her chair, allowing Jules the room he needed to select files from the drawer.

"Eenie, meenie, miney, mo," he joked while he ran his thumb across the tops of manila folders labeled with employee names. After lifting the four he needed, he said, "I really appreciate your cooperation, Micah. I will follow up with David and, of course, you with the results."

Micah closed the drawer and secured it. "Let me know what else, if anything, you'll need," she said, glancing at her watch as she stood and shook hands with Jules. As she walked out of the manager's area with him, she added, "I think I'll call it quits for the day. My fiancé's sister is in town and he's picking me up for an early dinner."

"Sounds good. Enjoy your evening." Jules patted her back before heading toward the HR offices.

"You too." Micah exited the back door, scanned the parking lot, and sighed aloud after seeing no signs of her vehicle. She'd loaned her car to Rossi that morning after Rossi had shared with her that his sister would be using his truck to begin her job search. She pulled out her cell and dialed Rossi's number.

"Hello," Rossi answered jovially after two rings, his voice overpowered by what sounded like chatter, laughter, music, and forks hitting plates. "No, no, that's not what I was saying!" He laughed boisterously. "Hold on a minute. . . . Hello," he started again.

"Where are you, Rossi?" Micah started feeling frustration creep in, recognizing that he was far from being on his way to pick her up.

"I'm up here at Macaroni Grill," he answered, still chuckling. "Romni and I were getting something to eat. Girl, you crazy," he said, talking to both Micah and Romni at the same time.

Immediately Micah was beside herself with fury. "First of all, Rossi, you were supposed to be picking me up right now!" she spat as she felt her eyes beginning to well with tears. "And secondly, we were supposed to go to dinner together. *To-ge-ther!* Do you have any concept of what that means!"

"Baby, I just lost track of time and forgot," Rossi exclaimed as innocently as he could.

"Why are you all the way in John Brown Dale City anyway!" Micah screamed, knowing that was the closest Macaroni Grill in the area, which was nearly an hour away. "And I'm sitting here with no

doggone way to get home while you are there with
my car feeding your damn face!"

"I'm on my way. Are you off already?" he asked,
still partially guffawing.

"You know what, Rossi, forget you!" she snarled.
"I'll find my own way home, but you better be
bringing me my keys right now!" She abruptly
ended the call, then with her hand pushed back
a sudden flow of tears that refused to obey her
will. After two minutes, she pulled herself together
and called Erin. "How late are you working tonight?" she asked.

"I was packing up to leave, why? I thought you
were going out to dinner," she replied.

"Yeah, that's what I thought too. I need a ride
home if you don't mind."

"What happened to y'all going out?" Erin asked,
perplexed.

"I'll tell you on the way home," Micah answered
dejectedly. "I'm out on the back patio."

"Okay, I'll be out as soon as I can. Give me about
fifteen minutes," Erin said.

Waiting on Erin, Micah examined every car that
passed through the lot, hoping against reality that
it would be Rossi pulling up with a small, black,
velvet box and an apology that sounded like: *I'm
sorry I'm late, baby; I really wasn't in Dale City. The jew-
eler was taking forever to get this cleaned. I had to cuss
him out for holding me up.* Her extremely wishful
thinking prompted her to look at her still-bare
ring finger. Minutes later, Erin emerged, then
hugged her friend after taking note of Micah's not
so pleasant expression. "Girl, what happened?"
she asked as they both piled their things into the
backseat of her car.

Micah went on a six-minute tirade that ended with, "I'm not ready to go home yet; stop at somebody's bar, 'cause I need a drink!"

"I don't see how or why you put up with him, Micah. I really don't. I'm not going to say too much because I know you love him, but I sure as heck can't figure out why." Erin shook her head.

The rest of the ride was silent other than Corinne Bailey Rae singing in her soft, melodious voice.

"Used to feel like heaven . . ."

When has this ever felt like heaven? Micah thought as she wiped away a stream of tears. *Is this the best a man who claims to love me can do?* While she couldn't help but become increasingly angry with Rossi, she became angry with herself for loving and considering marrying a man who seemed to care so little about her despite his constant confession of love. More questions invaded her thinking as more tears fell from her eyes. *Why don't I have a ring?* she thought, as she weighed Rossi's behaviors against the words of his mouth. *And why am I having to beg for a way home when I have a paid-for car? Why am I letting this man treat me like this? Am I that desperate?*

"This ain't love," she mumbled to herself with her face turned toward the window so Erin wouldn't hear her.

Erin parked her Accord on West Leigh Street, and the two ladies briskly walked to The Corner Bar & Grill. They quickly found seats and flagged a waitress over.

"I'll have a cosmopolitan made with orange juice instead of triple sec, and rim the glass with lemon juice please," Micah rambled off without thought as she dropped her keys and cell phone on the tabletop. Erin followed with a pink lady made with peach grenadine. The waitress walked off, freeing them to talk.

"Erin, I'm so angry right now I could blow that man's house up." Micah perused the menu for a full meal. "Here I am starving myself all day thinking we were going to dinner, and that fool ain't thought nothing about me at all." She rolled her eyes as she pressed her lips together. "I just don't understand what I'm doing so wrong."

"Girl, please, it's not you; it's him," she dismissed, with a wave of her hand. "So you still haven't met his sister?"

"Nope. It's like he's hiding her from me, or maybe hiding me from her. I've been trying to meet the girl all week! I would like to meet at least one in-law before the wedding!"

"But you're going to the family reunion next month, right? These chicken wings sound good. I think I'm going to have that."

"I'm supposed to be going, but damn, I don't know now," Micah said, slamming the menu on the table, then removing her suit jacket.

The waitress returned with their drinks. "What are you ladies having tonight?" Micah ordered a barbeque chicken breast entrée smothered in bourbon onions and grilled mushrooms topped with bacon, cheese, and parsley. She picked sweet mashed potatoes and sautéed vegetables as her sides, along with homemade cornbread, then surrendered her menu, convinced that she'd be pretty full at the end of the evening. "Great choice. And what about you, ma'am?" Erin chose pan-seared, marinated pork chops topped with an apple chutney sauce, accompanied by fried potatoes and green beans. "I'll have these right out," the waitress chirped and swished away.

"What do you think I should do? I mean, I don't have a ring, he's acting like a jack . . ." Her cell phone vibrating against the tabletop interrupted her sentence. Seeing Rossi's number flash across the screen, she quickly pressed the ignore key and threw the phone in her purse. "I can't talk to him right now." She shook her head in disgust, then focused back on Erin. "Anyway, what do you think I should do?"

"I don't know, Micah." She shrugged. "He could be waiting to present you with the ring at the reunion. I mean, he keeps saying that he wants to marry you, so I don't know. Maybe go to the reunion, but if he doesn't get down on one knee with a rock in his hand, then be done with it." She lifted her glass and sipped, then added, "It has to be that, because a man don't take just any ole body to meet his momma."

"I'm a little sick of giving him the benefit of the doubt. Why am I even doing all this planning? Did I tell you he wants to change the date?"

"What!" Erin nearly spat her drink on the table. "Why?"

"Talking about he needs to really press forward on his job and save some more money. I don't wanna hear that mess." The waitress reappeared with their entrees and placed them on the table. Right away the ladies dug in. "Can you imagine how stupid I feel having already told all of y'all and everybody at work and sent out my little 'save the date' e-mail announcements and all that? I would have sent one to his momma and sister, but neither of their backwoods-of-Georgia behinds have e-mail addresses. Now I gotta send a 'post-poned' e-mail."

"Why you send it without meeting his momma in the first place, girl! The parents are supposed to be the first to know," Erin chastised.

"Well, I can't force the man to take me home, can I? And the wedding was supposed to be just a few months from now. I didn't know he was going to come back and extend the date!" Micah said in her defense.

"What does he mean 'press on his job' anyway? Is it a money issue? Because if so, that's not such a bad idea. I mean, you do want the man to be able to take care of you," she said matter-of-factly.

"Yeah, I do, but you have to keep in mind that neither of us is in debt, and between the two of us we own two homes and make almost one hundred and fifty thousand dollars a year," Micah countered between bites of food. "And you know I'm not picky, Erin. I've not put any financial demands on Rossi."

"Maybe he owes the IRS back taxes and doesn't want to tell you."

"Maybe so, but if that's the case, you mean to tell me that we couldn't work through that together?"

"He might not want to put that kind of pressure on you going into a marriage, Micah," Erin said as she sank her teeth into a square of cornbread.

"Why are you taking up for him all of a sudden? First of all, him owing the IRS is hypothetical, and secondly, if it's true, he knew he owed the money before he sat up there and set the wedding date and watched me buy all this wedding stuff!" Micah stabbed her fork into her food. "You know what, I don't even want to talk about it anymore. I want to enjoy my dinner, just like he was doing tonight—without me!" she ranted, becoming more furious.

"So he didn't call or text or anything?" Erin confirmed once more.

"Didn't we already have that part of the discussion? I told you that on the way over here."

"He ought to be ashamed of himself," Erin replied, shaking her head.

"Now his sister has been here all week and I have yet to meet the woman. How is it that he plans to marry me but won't introduce me to his family?"

"Well, there is the family reunion. He did invite you to that."

"Yeah, he did."

"Well, like I said, maybe he is waiting until then to propose so he can do it in front of his whole family," Erin suggested again.

Micah's phone vibrated against the table a second time. She picked it up and pressed the keys to receive a text message.

Where r u? At da house w/ur truck n keys

She rolled her eyes but thumbed in a response letting him know she was out with Erin and to leave the keys inside the armrest.

"Hmph! I wouldn't have told him anything," Erin uttered. "He didn't think enough of you to pick up the phone and let you know where he was with your truck, and he stood you up in the process."

"Well, if I don't get a ring at this family reunion, I'm moving to Charlotte."

* * *

An hour later, Erin coasted along Micah's street and came to a stop in front of her home. As promised, her truck was parked in the driveway. Stuffed in the crack of the front door was a handwritten note from Rossi.

Thanks for all you do. You're the best. Love ya,
RE

She crumpled the note in her hand, let herself in the house, waved good-bye to Erin, and closed the door. Although she knew she was too frustrated to converse reasonably, she dialed Rossi's number on her cordless handset. He answered on the first ring, seemingly full of the same chuckles he'd been infected with earlier that evening.

"Hey, babe," he started.

"Rossi we need to talk," she started despondently as she headed up the stairs to her bedroom.

"Okay?" he said as if he had no clue of what could be egging her. "What's up?"

She let out an exasperated sigh before she started her next sentence. "I don't appreciate what you did tonight." She took a seat on the edge of her bed and slid her pumps off her tired feet.

"What are you talking about," he said, trying to brush her off.

"You know what I'm talking about, Rossi. How you stood me up and left me stranded tonight."

"I just ran behind on time, baby, that's all," he said lightly. "I'm sorry that I wasn't there to pick you up. I should have managed my time better."

"Why haven't I met your so-called sister?" she

spat. "She's been here all week and I have yet to meet her."

"We just been bumping heads with our schedules, that's all."

"All week?!" Micah shrieked. "She's been here all week and you couldn't find any time anywhere to let me meet your sister?"

"Baby, you've been working, I've been working, she's been job hunting. Time just ran short. I don't have any problem with you meeting her!" he exclaimed.

"I don't want to hear it, Rossi, because if you really wanted me to meet her, you would have made it happen. And then you had the audacity to not come pick me up from work?" she spat angrily as she began to remove her clothes.

"I said I was sorry for that. If I could go back and fix it I would, but I can't. I'm sorry, all right!" he huffed. "And look, if you want to meet my sister, we're having breakfast tomorrow before her flight leaves at eight. Why don't you come out and meet us," he offered.

"Oh, so now you expect me to be all happy and excited 'cause I'm forcing my way into your life? You know I have to work tomorrow morning." Now standing in just her panties and bra, she shuffled through a drawer of pajamas and pulled out her most comfortable pair, then took a seat on her bed again.

"You are not forcing your way; I want you in my life," he said, sounding more annoyed. "If I didn't, I wouldn't have even said it in the first place. We are going to be at Waffle House by the airport at six. You don't have to be at work until seven-thirty, and I would like for my sister and my fiancée to meet. Now if you decide not to come, that is on you. But I'm not gonna want to hear about it later if you don't," Rossi ended, effectively moving the ball to her court.

"Well, don't hold your damn breath!" she heaved before disconnecting the call and tossing the phone into a laundry basket full of clothes.

After taking a long hot shower trying to scrub away her anger, frustration, and disappointment, Micah padded back to her bed, collapsed against her pillows, and rolled her eyes as she set her clock for five A.M. to allow herself time to make breakfast.

Just a Prayer Away

Micah sat in the Waffle House alone for what seemed like forever waiting for Rossi and his sister to arrive. At least he did call to let her know they were running behind. She glanced down at her watch several times as twenty more minutes passed, but mostly kept her eyes affixed on the parking lot.

"Ma'am, you are going to have to order something or I'm going to have to ask you to leave, because we have too many people waiting." The waitress waved her hand around her to point out the number of waiting restaurant patrons.

"No problem." Micah gathered her work bag and purse, then stood to surrender the table. Just as she stepped out the door and headed for her car, Rossi's truck whipped into the parking lot but slowed as he maneuvered into an empty space. Right away he hopped out and walked briskly toward her.

"Micah, we aren't going to have time to do breakfast. Romni didn't pack until this morning." Micah's eyes glanced toward the passenger seat of

Rossi's truck and absorbed the features of the young lady who sat there. There was no denying that she was his twin, as they carried the same facial features, differentiated only by their genders. "I know you're mad, baby, but come on over here and meet my sister so I can get her on the plane."

Half of Micah wanted to spit in Rossi's face, but then she had to ask herself why she had expected anything different from what had taken place. His actions were typical and predictable. Being honest, she admitted internally that had Rossi shown up on time, it would have shocked her. She followed Rossi with less than anxious steps.

Seeing the two approach, Romni hopped out of her brother's vehicle with a wide smile on her face. Before Rossi could make an introduction, she extended her hand.

"Hi, I'm Romni."

"Micah," she exchanged pleasantly.

"Romni, Micah. Micah, this is my baby twin sister, Romni," Rossi said, then grabbed Romni and pressed his lips against her cheek and rocked her back and forth as he laughed.

"You're only two minutes older than me," she shrieked with giggles, trying to push him away.

"And that's enough to make you my baby sister."

Micah stood watching their playful sibling banter, their love for each other evident. She couldn't think of a time when Rossi had expressed his love for her so openly. Even now, she noticed how he had introduced her only by name, giving her no title. She forced a smile on her face while the pair palled around for a few more seconds.

"Let me get you to your plane," Rossi ended, finally letting go of his twin.

"It was nice meeting you, Micah," Romni said as she extended her arms toward Micah for a hug. "I'll be moving up here soon. Maybe we can do lunch or hang out together or something."

Micah accepted the gesture, patting Romnie on the back twice during the light embrace. "That sounds great. It was nice meeting you as well, even though you have to rush off. How soon will you be relocating here?"

"Right after our family reunion in a couple of weeks, right, Rossi?"

"Yep! I can't wait, sis." Rossi wrapped his arms around his sister a second time.

"Okay, well have a safe trip back home," Micah finished, becoming more envious of Rossi's display of open affection, which he'd never expressed with her. "I should be off early tonight, Rossi," she added.

"All right," he stated, giving her what she considered a church hug, which equated to a single fully extended arm and two pats on the back. "I'll call you later."

"Yeah, right," Micah spoke more to herself than to Rossi.

As soon as Romni entered her home, she wished she could turn around and go back to Richmond. T-Dog greeted her with a punch to the jaw and an effort to snatch a fistful of hair from her head. He blurted obscenities as he landed blows to her face and stomach.

"Where was you at! Huh?" he questioned as she begged him to stop. "You speck me to believe you was at your brother's house?"

"T, please stop!" she cried out, throwing her

arm up to shield her face. "I told you I was at Rossi's house!"

"And you couldn'tna told me that while you were there? Much as you like to run your mouth on the damn phone, you couldn'tna called me?" He wrapped his hands around her neck. "'Cause your ass won't over there!" he spat, tightening his grip. Romni grappled at his strong hands desperately trying to free herself. In just a few seconds with no oxygen supply, she weakened and her eyes began to roll to the back of her head. Sudden knocking on the door caused T-Dog to instantly let go of Romni and shove his hands into his pockets. "Who is it?!" he yelled.

"It's Crystal. I brought you something to eat." Crystal had been cooking and sleeping with T-Dog while Romni had been away after he'd convinced her that he'd put Romni out.

"I'll be over in a minute." T-Dog cut his eyes over at Romni, who lay crumpled on the floor coughing and holding her neck. He bent down and forcefully grabbed her chin. "You best be in this house when I get back," he fired. She nodded quickly before he all but slammed her head back into the tile floor and then walked out the door.

Lying in a heap, Romni cried for the next hour, although her welcome was nothing short of what she'd expected. Nonetheless, both her physical and emotional pain immobilized her, holding her captive to the small area of cold tiles. "Lord, please help me get myself together," she spoke softly and sincerely. "I know I haven't always done the right thing, but even so, I know you have better for me than this, God." Her tears began to flow more rapidly as she spoke from her soul. "You do have something else for me, right? I know I've messed up, God. Right now I'm living with this man and I know you aren't happy about that, but with your help, I'm willing and ready to make a change, Lord. I'm ready to clean up. I just need one word from you, God. Just something to let me know that you still love me and that you still hear my prayers." As the last word left Romni's lips, her tears began to slow and gradually she felt strength creeping into her weary frame.

She gathered herself up and rose to her feet, then through her pain took careful and measured steps to her bedroom. She stopped in the doorway, discouraged, as she scanned the mess her bedroom was in. The bed hadn't been made, though clearly slept in. An array of adult magazines were scattered across the worn sheet, which left a large portion of a dingy mattress exposed. Beer cans and bottles lay on their sides along with condom wrappers, a few used condoms, and various bags and trash from fast-food chains. Laundry still needed to be done and lay wherever there was space on the floor minus a wide pathway that led from the bedroom door to the bed. A collection of CDs shared the floor space in front of a small portable CD player whose speakers had been detached and positioned on both sides of the mattress at the foot of the bed. Three ashtrays full of burned cigarette butts, one ashtray overturned, sat on the dresser next to an uneven stack of dirty plates made topsy-turvy by the forks that were inserted between each one.

Romni sighed aloud, then repeated to God, "I said I'm ready to clean up." Without wasting any time, she headed for the kitchen, frowned at the mess that had been left there as well, then dug in the cabinet beneath the sink, grabbed a handful of grocery store bags, and headed back to her room.

First lifting the CDs from the floor, she sorted through a few as she stacked them against each other in her hand, then stopped when she came across a burned copy of *Yolanda Adams Live in Washington.* Knowing the anointed voice and lyrics of the dynamic artist would give her the encouragement and motivation she needed, she quickly inserted the CD into the player and boosted the volume.

Inspired by the upbeat pace of the first track, Romni began collecting trash and cleaning up as she sang the few lyrics she knew. By the time she reached the fourth track, the room had begun to look like sleeping quarters again. Romni stood still as more tears filled her eyes when Yolanda passionately sang the lyrics of a song that reached her very soul.

"Out of everyone who loves you, I your Father love you the most! . . . I am just a prayer away. . . ."

"Thank you," Romni whispered as she looked at the ceiling. "Thank you!"

With renewed strength and encouragement, Romni finished cleaning her room, took the trash to the Dumpster, and stacked a few baskets of laundry by the front door that she planned on washing in the morning. Next she showered until the water turned cold as she made a to-do list in her mind of steps she would take to clean up her life, which she knew she could do with God's help.

"Thanks for going with me today," Charvette said as Victori plopped in the passenger side of the two-seater BMW.

"No problem, girl. I want to see this man you keep raving about."

"Hopefully, he won't be home when we get there."

"Oh yeah, that's right," Victori replied, snapping her fingers. "Stop somewhere so I can get something to eat," she instructed. "We have time."

It was shortly after ten in the morning when Charvette pulled onto I-95 north headed for Fredericksburg on a mission to find out if Kinston and Naomi were back together. Dressed in long skirts, modest blouses, pantyhose, and plain pumps, the two women giggled on their way up the highway until Charvette reached exit 130B and stopped at Denny's for breakfast.

"I can't believe you got me out here looking like I'm about to go to choir rehearsal," Victori said, lifting herself from the car seat, which was just a few inches from the ground. "And why did you drive this?! This car doesn't match our image."

"I wasn't thinking, Sister Victori," Charvette said with a laugh as she locked the doors. Then they headed inside the restaurant.

Charvette enjoyed a ham and scrambled egg sandwich with Swiss and American cheese grilled on sourdough bread, along with a side of grits, while Victori had her way with a scrambled egg dish featuring chopped bacon, country-fried potatoes, green peppers and onions, topped with cheddar cheese, sided with two sausage links, hash browns, and three fluffy buttermilk pancakes.

"Did you remember to bring your Bible?" Charvette stirred several packets of sugar into a glass of tea.

"Yeah, it's in my purse. I found some old magazines, too, that we can use."

"Good. I never keep those things."

Once the ladies filled their bellies they headed back for the car and drove to a neighborhood of million-dollar homes on Wateredge Lane.

"Homeboy lives back here?" Victori exclaimed, impressed with the homes and the acreage of each lot.

"Yep. He makes good money," Charvette said, with a nod, as she eased the car to a stop a few houses down from Kinston's home.

"Are you sure he's not home?"

"He's not supposed to be. But if he is, me coming shouldn't be a problem if he is still living by himself, right?"

"Well, you got a point there, but how are you going to explain me coming with you and these glad rags we got on."

"He's not home, Victori. He's out of town," Charvette stated assuredly. "All right, get your Bible in your hand and let's go." While Charvette had opened her front door many times to shoo away Jehovah's Witnesses, for the life of her, she couldn't remember what they said as an opening line, but convinced that she'd think of something, she trodded onward with Victori beside her.

Together they approached Kinston's door and rang the bell. Charvette nearly fell over backward when a tall, thin but shapely woman whose physical features and intricately braided hair could have easily classified her as an African goddess answered the door.

"May I help you?" she asked. Right away Charvette recognized her voice from the message Kinston had played for her months before.

"Hi, ma'am. Uh, we uh . . . we were just stopping by to share the good news of the Gospel with you this morning," she said, struggling for words. "Do you have a few minutes?" she asked nervously, expecting the woman to dismiss them.

"Sure. Come on in," she offered, widening the door's opening.

"Great!" Charvette stepped through the door into the foyer as she had done several times in the past, but under very different circumstances. "My name is Cha—Sharon," she stuttered, "and this is Vanessa."

"I'm Naomi. Nice to meet you."

"This is a beautiful home you have here," Victori acknowledged, looking around at the beautifully painted walls, columns, and furnishings.

"Thank you. My husband surprised me with it when we came back from our honeymoon a couple of years ago."

"Oh, so you're married?" Victori asked, with a smile. "That is so wonderful. I hope to get married someday, but I just haven't found the right man, I guess."

And neither have I, Charvette thought as she fought back tears.

Naomi nodded. "Well, we've been married for five years now, and I can say it hasn't always been pretty but we've been able to hold it together. You ladies can have a seat." She pointed with her hand toward the living room. "Can I get you something to drink?"

"Some water please," Charvette managed to say.

"Yes, water would be great."

Naomi disappeared into the kitchen, freeing Charvette and Victori to whisper.

"So he *is* back with her," Charvette started.

"I guess, she walking around like she lives here."

"I can't believe this."

"Well, you'd better be thinking about what you are going to say out of that Bible you have in your lap."

Charvette's eyes stretched wide. "I don't know anything about how to do this!"

"You'd better think of something quick."

Naomi returned with two glasses and set them on the coffee table atop coasters. With a pleasant smile she sat, welcoming the ladies to begin witnessing.

Suddenly remembering the Watchtower publications Victori had stashed in her purse, Charvette motioned that the purse be handed to her. "Basically we just wanted to share this booklet with you." She took a publication from Victori's purse and glanced at the cover. "Um . . . the Bible says that God's will be done on earth as it is in heaven, so one day, we are going to live forever on earth." Charvette's fingers trembled as she thumbed through a few pages looking for a picture she'd seen a thousand times of a lion and a lamb lying together amid luscious green grass, trees, and baskets overflowing with fresh fruit and vegetables. Luckily she found what she'd been searching for toward the back, folded the booklet in half, and presented it to Naomi. "Wouldn't you like to live in a place like this, where there is just peace and harmony?" she asked in a quivering voice.

"Yes, that looks pretty nice, but I'm looking forward to living my afterlife in heaven, where the streets are paved with gold," Naomi answered.

"Oh."

"Because in the word of God, Jesus said that He was going away to prepare a place for us, and if it were not so, He would have told us," Naomi answered with confidence.

At a complete loss, all Charvette could do was nod her head.

"We'd like to leave this booklet with you to read in your spare time," Victori injected as a save. "Is that okay?"

"I guess I could take a look at some of the articles," Naomi said, reaching for the information. When she did, Charvette rose to her feet.

"Thank you for your time and letting us come in and share," Charvette said, handing the outdated publication to her lover's wife with trembling hands.

"Thanks for stopping by." Naomi walked the ladies to the door and saw them out.

They walked in silence until they reached Charvette's BMW and got inside.

"So there you have it. They're back together . . . that is, if they ever broke up," Victori said.

With downward-turned lips, Charvette just shook her head and nudged away a few tears.

"So what are you gonna do?"

"I don't know," Charvette answered just above a whisper. "I love that man." She slammed her head against the headrest and stared at the ceiling of her car. "I can't believe this." She pressed her lips together in silence for nearly a minute. "I'm going to have to let him go."

These Are My Confessions

Dressed for work, Gideon knocked on Erin's front door after not hearing from her for a solid week. She opened momentarily, dressed in a small pair of denim shorts and a white fitted T-shirt. A red and white bandana covered her hair, signifying that she was in the middle of cleaning. She twisted her lips at the sight of him but let him in without uttering a single word.

"Hello to you, too," Gideon commented as he crossed the threshold into her apartment. "I didn't sleep with you last night," he added, which was his way of saying she hadn't said good morning.

"Who did you sleep with?" Erin asked dryly. She returned to the kitchen, where she'd just finished scrubbing the floor.

"What are you talking about? I slept by myself, like I always do, Erin."

"Yeah, right." She purposely bent at the waist,

giving Gideon a nice view of what he'd come over for but wouldn't be getting. With his nature now raised, he saddled up behind her resting his hands at her waist.

"Mmm, girl," he moaned as he pushed his hips forward. "I'll sleep with you right now, though."

"Oh no you won't, either. Not until you tell me why that woman coming out of your house the other night," Erin challenged as she turned to face him. The stern look on her face demanded that he start explaining.

"Who are you talking about, baby?" he huffed as he leaned back against the kitchen counter.

"You know good and well who I'm talking about, Gideon, and I don't appreciate you standing up here trying to make a fool out of me. I saw her coming out of your house!" she fired.

"You saw who coming out when?" he asked, feigning utter confusion, although he clearly remembered Anjaneen straddling across him a few nights before. Just the thought of her caused his manhood to leap inside his pants.

"Okay, so I'm stupid, right?"

"I'm not calling you stupid, Erin; I'm asking you to tell me what you're talking about."

"You know what? Get your lying, conniving ass outta my house," she spat, standing firm in her kitchen.

"Baby, stop acting like that," he pressed. "I came over here to see you before I went to work because I haven't seen you all week. I don't feel like arguing."

"And I don't feel like hearing you lie to me, Gideon."

"Lie to you about what? I told you I . . . ohhhh!" he eased, snapping his fingers as if Anjaneen had just entered his recollection. He chuckled to make himself more believable. "Okay, okay. I know who you're talking about now."

"Oh, do you?" Erin pressed her lips together tightly, unmoved by his sudden improvement in memory.

"You talking about Ann," he said careful not to call her full name. "Baby, that's nothing." Erin only stared with piercing eyes. "I'm going to tell you exactly what happened," he started, then sighed, realizing that Erin wasn't even about to let it go. "Ann is my ex-girlfriend. When we were seeing each other I had given her a key and I never got it back when we broke up. She came over the other day unannounced and let herself in when I wasn't even home." Gideon paused pensively, grappling for words that he could only hope would prevent any damage being done to the good thing he had going with his woman. "By the time I got there, she was waiting for me in my bedroom with no clothes on." He looked down at his feet and shook his head with a shameful chuckle. "I'm not going to lie to you, Erin; I was tempted. *Very* tempted. And we did kiss, but I told her she had to leave right then." He bit into his lip and searched Erin's eyes for a hint of forgiveness but saw none. "Nothing happened," he said adamantly. "Nothing at all. Now she did try, but I couldn't do that to you," he ended, reaching for her hand, but Erin snatched it away.

"Do you know how ridiculous you sound?"

"I'm trying to be honest. I'm coming clean with you, Erin. I need you to hear me. I need you to believe me," he said, almost starting to beg.

"So you want to convince me that this woman you used to see comes to your house with her very own key, lets herself in, gets butt-bald naked, gets in your bed, and waits for you to come home." Erin tapped her fingers against her pressed lips and thought for a few seconds. "You come in the apartment, go to your bedroom, see her lying there, get hard, then tell her to get out. She gets dressed . . . wait; do you watch her get dressed?" she interrogated.

"I . . . I," Gideon stumbled over his next words, not sure which answer would be deemed the most appropriate and believable. "I left out the room because I know how Ann is. She would have been all over me if I would have stayed in there, so I sat down in the living room and started watching the game until she came out."

"So your answer is no, you didn't watch her get dressed, then."

"No, I didn't, baby," Gideon answered, which wasn't a lie; indeed, he had not watched Anjaneen redress herself. "After I told her she had to get out of there, she came out dressed a few minutes later, and then I walked her to the door. I did kiss her, but I swear to you, that's all that happened," he promised, holding both hands up in the air. "I never took my clothes off."

"Did you have the sense to use a condom?!" she roared, not believing his plea of innocence.

"Didn't have to. Nothing happened," he repeated. "She came out the room, I walked her to her car, and on the way I got caught up in a moment of stupidity and kissed her, but that was it," he said calmly without shifting his eyes left or right. Erin studied his eyes intently for a full three minutes. Other than blink, Gideon never took his eyes off her. "I'm sorry, Erin," he finally spoke, reaching for her a second time.

"You're sorry?" she asked incredulously, although

her hand rested lifelessly inside his. "You gave this woman a key to your house so she could come and go as she pleased, then you had your hands and lips all over her, you turn around and lie when I ask you about her, and 'I'm sorry' is supposed to fix it?"

Internally Gideon sighed in relief, sensing forgiveness on the horizon "I know a simple apology doesn't even begin to undo the damage. I've broken your trust and I've hurt you," he said as meekly as he could. "I was stupid, baby, but I didn't sleep with her." He begged her forgiveness with his eyes. "You have my heart, Erin, and you're the only woman I want." Slowly he dropped to one knee, then lowered the other so that he knelt at her feet. "Baby, please believe me."

"Does she still have the key?"

"No. Well, yes, she still has it, but I had my locks changed the very next day." Pleased with himself, he dug into his pocket and retrieved a duplicate key for the new lock that he'd had installed once he'd determined that somehow Erin knew something. "She doesn't have a key anymore—only you do," he said further. As he spoke those last words, he slid his hand into his alternate pocket and pulled out a long velvet box. He opened it to reveal a sparkling sterling silver filigree charm bracelet featuring a heart-shaped lock and a skeleton key encrusted with diamond accents. "And you're the only woman with the key to my heart and my soul."

Erin stood silently surprised as Gideon fastened the jewelry around her wrist, then kissed both the back and palm of her hand as he looked up at her face with eyes filled with remorse. For good measure he forced a tear to trickle down as he tugged slightly on her arm, beckoning her toward him.

With a hint of reluctance, Erin lowered herself to her knees, meeting Gideon eye to eye. Instantly he wrapped his arms tightly around her and expressed his regret in a string of mumbled words over and over again. Cautiously he began placing light kisses from her neck up to her jaw, her chin, and then her lips. He pecked three times, delicately measuring her level of reception, and when she met his lips with just a slight touch of her tongue, he knew all things had been forgiven. Quickly his kisses became more sensual and his hands began to roam her body as he felt her anger subsiding and her defenses weakening.

   Moments later they lay collapsed in each other's arms in the middle of Erin's freshly mopped kitchen floor.

All You Need
Is a Little Bitta This

Old-school jams surrounded the patrons of Platinum 112, the club where the girls chose to spend their evening, feeling like the crew from an old episode of *Girlfriends*.

"I'll be back; I'm going to the little girls' room," Micah said, then slid from the rounded booth after she took another sip from her glass. As she tipped to the back hallway, she noticed a pair of eyes belonging to a tall brother with smooth round locks dressed in all black. When their eyes caught, she gave him a sliver of a smile but never broke her stride. He returned the gesture with a slight head tilt, then turned away to the bar.

"Now that's someone I wouldn't mind doing a little two-step and having some dinner with," she commented to herself. In that instant, she was reminded of Rossi backing out of dinner yet again, claiming that one of his managers had called in sick. Hearing the chiming of her cell phone, she opened her purse, fished for it, and pulled it out to read the incoming text from Rossi.

Sorry about tonite—can you still bring me something to eat?

She winced, then rolled her eyes as she dropped the phone back into her purse. "I wish I would bring your so-and-so something," she mumbled. Not paying attention where she was going, she took two steps and bumped into a man's solid chest. "Oh, I'm sor—" Her words stopped immediately as she looked up into the face of none other than Anthony McDonald. Right away she tried to sidestep him, forgoing the apology that she would have freely given to anyone else.

Anthony snatched Micah by the arm and spun her to him with a smug look on his face. "Oh, you can't say excuse me?"

"Let go of me, Anthony," she said through clenched teeth as she attempted to pull away.

"See, I know what your problem is. You think you a strong black woman and can't nobody mess with you. Thinking you run things and all that," he said facetiously. "But what you really need is somma this right here," he said, grabbing his crotch and thrusting his hips forward in rapid succession. He chuckled as he let her go with a shove, then turned and walked off toward his own table.

Stunned, perplexed, and infuriated to the point of tears, Micah quickly visited the ladies' room, then rejoined her friends. Right away Erin noticed her grim expression.

"What the monkey happened to you?" she exclaimed.

"That fool!" Micah spat with her eyes narrowed into slits that barely let her tears escape. Before they could trail down her face she smeared them up into her hairline. "What did I do to deserve having to deal with him!"

"Who are you talking about?"

"Anthony McDonald. I just ran into him on my way to the bathroom." Micah picked up her glass and gulped down the remainder of her drink, then repeated Anthony's comment.

"Girl, you need a restraining order for that nut," Erin exclaimed.

"My head is starting to hurt," Micah said, reaching for her temples. Her thoughts were scattered and rolling around inside her head like marbles. Anthony's words and gestures played over and over in her head until she could no longer hear the conversation at the table or even the music, although it blared from the speakers. After twenty more minutes of sitting and staring blankly, she grabbed for her purse and headed back for the ladies' room to splash water on her face. "I'll be right back," she announced.

"I'll come with you," Charvette offered.

"No. I'm good." In an instant, she clicked her way toward the back of the club but was stopped by the brother whom she'd noticed earlier.

"Excuse me, are you all right?" he asked.

"Yes, I'm fine, thank you."

"You sure? You look a little troubled. Can I buy you a drink, or at least lend you a listening ear?"

"No, thank you. I'm about to leave in a few minutes," Micah politely replied as she caught a glimpse of his deep, soulful eyes. "Excuse me," she added, trying to quickly maneuver around him but stumbling in her haste.

"Watch yourself, beautiful." The gentleman caught her by the arm and helped her regain her balance.

"Thanks," Micah said as her lips formed a partial smile.

"Can I at least walk you to your car? I'm Stephen Rashaud, by the way."

Micah paused for two seconds before accepting his offer for a handshake, although she'd practically fallen into his arms just seconds before. "Micah," she said, smiling a little more. "I guess you can see me to my car; just let me get a couple of my girls." She turned back toward the table but then turned again abruptly to look Stephen directly in the eyes. "Let me just say that once I get to my car, I'm getting inside and driving off; no hugs, no kiss, no phone number exchange," she said with finality.

"I'm just trying to be a gentleman," Stephen said, with a slow shrug, turning his lips downward. "No hugs, no kiss, no number exchanges," he agreed.

"Be right back." Micah, not having a reason to be anxious, took her time stepping toward her friends. Victori was out on the dance floor breaking a little bit of a sweat, while Charvette and Erin nursed their drinks.

"Can you two walk me to my car with this dude back here?" Micah motioned her head, causing both ladies to dart their eyes Stephen's way.

"Yeah, girl. Wait until Victori gets back, though, to watch these drinks. You know how people do," Charvette commented.

Two minutes later, Victori panted back to the table and practically collapsed. "Whoo! That's my song right there!" She noticed the ladies with their purses in hand. "Y'all 'bout to leave?"

"We're just walking Micah out. Watch the drinks."

"Micah, don't let that joker Anthony worry you to death. You've already lost ten pounds behind him and his mess," Victori huffed before sipping from her glass. "I'll be right here."

"I'll call you tomorrow," Micah ended before making her way back to where Stephen stood, while Charvette and Erin trailed a few steps behind.

"I'm ready." Micah barely even looked at him as she pretended to be preoccupied with digging her keys out of her purse. The truth was she didn't want to give him any reason to think his taking a quick stroll down the sidewalk would lead to anything else, just in case he was a little hopeful. Not even waiting for him to escort her, she beelined for the door in front of him. Saying nothing, Stephen took even strides easily catching her before she reached the exit, then extended his arm in front of her to push the door open and held it for the three ladies.

Although Stephen strode with her, the two-minute walk to Micah's truck was silent. Stephen easily recognized that something was wrong and was careful not to be invasive and make Micah uncomfortable. And Micah simply had too much on her mind to know where to begin if she chose to say anything at all. All that could be heard was Erin and Charvette chattering about one of Charvette's clients.

A quick beep of her horn triggered by her fingering the keyless entry remote signaled Stephen that they'd reached her truck.

"Thanks for walking me," she blurted, rushing to the driver's side and reaching for the door handle.

"Let me get that for you, Ms. Micah." Stephen opened the door and let her get settled inside. "Drive safe now." He closed the door, took a few steps back, and stood as she slowly pulled away in front of him. He tapped the truck with his hand and then turned to walk back into the club, but not before trying to eke a little information from whichever one of Micah's friends would spill the beans.

"I'll see you ladies safely back inside," he offered.

"Oh, that won't be necessary," Erin quickly replied.

"It would be my pleasure, since we're all going back inside." Again, his long legs worked in his favor. "I'm Stephen, by the way." Charvette raised a suspicious eyebrow, while Erin responded in order.

"Nice to meet you, I guess."

"Do you all come here often?" When they responded only with a slight shrug he decided to just cut to the chase. "Let me just be straightforward. I couldn't help but notice your friend Micah, but unfortunately, she left before I could really get a chance to talk to her."

"I know you don't expect us to give you her phone number," Charvette quipped.

"No, not at all, but what I was hoping for was, you could tell me when you all are planning on coming back here so I can see her again." He hoped for a favorable response.

"I tell you what," Erin said, chuckling, "why don't you just come every night and see what night we show up. Why don't you try that?"

Stephen didn't find her sarcasm amusing but knew he had no choice but to accept it if he wanted to stay in their good graces in case he should ever see them out again. "I guess nothing beats a failure but a try." No sooner than he opened the club doors, Erin and Charvette darted to their table. "You ladies have a good night," he said, trying to give the adieu of a respectable gentleman, but his words were immediately drowned out by the blaring music.

Infuriated, Micah dialed Rossi's numbers repeatedly but got no answer. She blurted message after message through her anger instructing him to call her as soon as the message was received, then held the phone in her palm waiting for his reply. By the time she pulled into her driveway, she'd left a total of ten messages on his cell and home phones.

When she woke two hours later, the clock read 1:19 A.M.; she still held the phone in her hand with no calls missed. She dialed Rossi's number once more and still got no answer. Certain that he'd received her previous messages, she hung up even more angry and frustrated than she'd been hours earlier. Another hour passed before she got a hold of him.

"Rossi, I need to talk to you and I'm on my way over there right now," Micah spoke into her cell phone as soon as she woke up. Her anger was refueled by both her thoughts of Anthony's actions and the fact that Rossi had not returned her phone calls despite her multiple messages.

"What's wrong, baby," he said, his voice nearly

drowned out by George Clooney's voice giving instruction to the other actors of *Ocean's Thirteen*.

"I'll tell you when I get there."

"You coming over here now? It's two-thirty in the morning. What's this about?" Rossi sat slumped on his couch, only half listening, his attention divided between Micah's call and his television screen.

"I'll be there in a few minutes."

"All right," Rossi dismissed. "I'll unlock the door."

Micah replayed Anthony's comment in her head. "Why does this man hate me so much," she uttered above the truck radio.

Micah arrived and let herself in; though Rossi heard her enter, he didn't bother to stand and greet her, keeping his eyes glued to the screen. "Hey," he spoke never turning to look her way.

Micah stood silently in the foyer waiting for Rossi, who knew she was upset, to be more attentive. After waiting several seconds to no avail, she stomped over to the television, fumbled for the power button on the set's front, turned it off, then took a defiant stance in front of him. Rossi only sighed, rather than make a big deal over Micah interrupting the movie.

"Rossi, did you hear me come in the door?" She folded her arms across her chest.

"Yeah, babe," he said as he rose to his feet and collected an empty soda can and a large bag of opened potato chips. "What's up?" Dragging his feet in a pair of Adidas Mungo shower shoes, he jerked the waistline of his basketball shorts, pulling them up for only a split second before they resettled around his hips again, as he headed for the kitchen.

Micah chewed on her bottom lip, trying to keep

her composure. "I must be invisible," she started, following closely behind Rossi. "Because I came in the door, but you didn't greet me."

"I did so," he disagreed. "I said hey as soon as you walked in the door."

"And I guess that was supposed to be enough, huh?"

"Listen, I don't feel like fussing and arguing tonight. Just tell me what happened and skip all this other drama," he said, becoming quickly exasperated.

"You know what, Rossi?" She shook her head as anger began to rise inside her. "I don't know any other man who claims he loves somebody and treats them so poorly. You suck," she mumbled.

Rossi rolled the bag of chips and attached a large spring clip to keep the bag closed, then walked over to her. "You need to stop being so spoiled. The world doesn't start and stop on your command." Now standing breath to breath, he draped his arms around her waist. "Now what happened?"

"You sure you don't want to finish watching your movie? I mean, this is the one and only time you will ever get to see this particular scene," Micah shot sarcastically.

"Go 'head, baby," he coaxed, paying no mind to her attitude.

She rolled her eyes, then began. "I saw that idiot Anthony in Platinum tonight." Micah paused as she stepped back and stared intently into Rossi's eyes. "And he said something that really . . . really offended me."

"Which was what, babe?" he shrugged, staring back at her.

"He grabbed me by my arm and told me what I

needed was 'somma this right here,'" she shot, mimicking Anthony's gesture.

Rossi's eyebrows instantly shot up. "He put his hands on you?"

"I just told you he grabbed me by my arm."

"This fool put his hands on you?" Rossi asked again more as a statement than a question.

"Yes, Rossi, and said what I needed was . . ." Before Micah could repeat herself, Rossi had jerked away and headed toward his front door, where he'd taken off his shoes. Quickly he slipped into a pair of black K-Swiss, then headed for his bedroom. "What are you doing?" Micah asked, practically chasing him up the stairs.

"This is the same cat who has been harassing you at work, right?" Rossi asked rhetorically as he shuffled past a few shoeboxes on his closet shelf until the one he wanted rested in his hands.

"Yeah, it's the same guy."

"I'm 'bout to put a stop to his madness by putting a cap in his ass," he said with almost no inflection in his voice tone. "'Cause he don't have no business putting his hands on you," he ended, looking directly at Micah for a few seconds, then back at the nine millimeter he held in his right hand.

"What are you going to do?" Rossi didn't respond with words, but instead dug in the box for the weapon's magazine, checked it for bullets, then slid it into the handle. "Rossi, please don't do anything stupid." In nervous reaction, Micah ran her fingers through her hair and held her head.

"Watch out, babe," he said, pushing past her, then bounding down the steps two at a time. "I'll be back." In an instant he was on the ground floor with his keys in his hand and headed out the door. Micah, who wasn't quite as agile on the stairs, still dressed in her stilettos and club attire, stumbled to catch up with Rossi but was several seconds behind.

"Rossi, wait!" she called after him to no avail.

In a fit of anger, Rossi skidded down the street, leaving Micah standing on his front porch confused. As he slowed at an intersection to prevent completely disregarding a stop sign, he took a moment to tuck the gun under his seat. Driving in dead silence and nearly running every traffic light, Rossi sped toward the highway ramp, pulled onto it, and merged between a couple of approaching vehicles.

The buzzing of his cell phone interrupted his thoughts. "What, Micah?" he answered in a calm yet irritated tone.

"Where are you going?" she asked, sounding almost panic-stricken.

"Going to take care of some business."

"Rossi, please don't do anything stupid," Micah begged.

"Stupid like what? I told you—he ain't have no business putting his hands on you. A man doesn't let another man touch his woman and do nothing about it," he answered, pressing more into the gas pedal. "Go ahead home, Micah. Don't worry about me. I'ma handle my business. Trust me, the less you know, the better off you are."

"Baby, please. Just don't . . ."

"I'll call you later." Rossi pressed the end button on his phone and dropped it in the passenger seat, then cranked up his stereo, shifted gears, and sped off into the night.

Continually peeping out Rossi's bedroom window at the faintest sound of a passing car, Micah attempted to wait for Rossi to return. It only took an hour for her to throw in the towel with her fight against her heavy eyelids. She laid across Rossi's bed right at three in the morning, and when she woke again, Rossi lay beside her in only his boxers with his arm draped across her waist. His gun lay on the nightstand alongside his wallet and keys. She sat up slowly so as not to disturb him and scanned his body for scratches, bruises, blood, or any other indication of a scuffle. Finding nothing, she sighed in relief that he'd made it home safely, although she had no clue what had taken place over the last couple of hours.

She nestled into his chest, and feeling her stir beside him, Rossi turned toward her and pulled her more into himself.

"What's wrong, babe?" he mumbled without opening his eyes.

"Nothing," she whispered. "I'm just glad you're okay." A few seconds passed before she added, "I love you, Rossi."

"Mm-hmm, love you too," he mumbled as he quickly pecked the top of her head, then drifted back to sleep.

The Power to Choose

Charvette sat in her office after hours completing her daily business housekeeping routine, recording services performed and money collected. It had been an extremely busy Tuesday, but Charvette found no reason to complain. She checked the appointment book for the next day and sighed in relief, as her first client wasn't scheduled to arrive until after twelve. That would give her an opportunity to sleep in a little and try to get some shopping done.

She rose from her seat with a pad in her hand and headed for the supply closet to take a quick inventory and complete her supply reorder form. Startled by quick rapping on the shop's door, Charvette grabbed her chest but quickly smiled as she recognized Kinston's face peering through the glass. He held a huge bouquet of flowers in one hand and a picnic basket in the other, waiting patiently for Charvette to let him in.

"Man, you scared me to death!" She slapped him on the arm as he walked through the shop's doors, then wasted no time tumbling the locks back over to secure the building.

"I had to come see about my baby," he said, setting the basket on the receptionist counter, then gathering Charvette tightly into a single arm. "I haven't had a chance to do this"—he gingerly joined his lips to hers—"in about two weeks," he whispered, then lowered his head a second time to cover her mouth with his.

Charvette struggled in her thoughts whether to confront him with what she'd found out, or to enjoy the warmth of his hands, lips, and body. She bit her lip as she studied his eyes for a few seconds. "Kinston, I need to ask you something," she started.

"Well ask me later, baby, because right now, all I want to do is spoil you." Kinston handed her the arrangement of flowers, a dazzling bouquet of exotic deep purple Singapore orchids. "These are for you."

"These are beautiful," she said, taking the group of thirty stems from his hand.

"And you are beautiful. Do you have something to put them in?"

"I'm sure I can find something." Charvette walked to the back of the shop and opened a few cabinets until she found a vase that had been idling there since her shop's grand opening more than three years ago. By the time she filled the vase with water and returned to the front of the shop, Kinston had covered the table in the waiting area with a tablecloth and set up and lit several tea light candles. A romantic ambiance took over the shop while he pulled out two chicken salad croissants, a large cluster of grapes, and two prepackaged salads. Seeing the setup, Charvette turned on her heels toward the stereo in the corner and set the dial to the smooth jazz station.

Kinston stood to embrace her as Al Jarreau's "So Good" emitted from the speakers. Slowly they danced in each other's arms, although they barely moved their feet at all.

"This feels so good, baby," Kinston whispered. "So good." His breathing became slightly heavier as he nuzzled Charvette's neck, working through her defenses. As the song came to an end, he led her to the couch, which was generally filled with waiting patrons, and they enjoyed dinner while Kinston updated her on his progression at work. Charvette's recent visit to his home still egged at her, but her emotions of love took precedent, further fired by the longing she felt between her thighs.

Tonight will be the last time, she told herself as they cleaned up after their meal. Then they left the shop and headed for her home.

Kinston snuggled against Charvette's back and planted kisses on her neck and shoulders. "Mmm," he moaned. "Baby, you're so good to me," he whispered in her ear. "Let's go for round three," he suggested.

"Kinston, what are you doing here?" she asked, tightening his arms around her as if they were a blanket.

"Making love to my baby," he whispered as he squeezed her breasts. "You know you're my baby, right?"

Charvette winced, although they had spent the last two hours tangled in each other's limbs and exploring each other's body with wet, passionate kisses. But now that the heat of the moment had passed—again—reality kicked in. "Why didn't you tell me you and Naomi were back together?"

"What? Where did you get that notion?" he denied in his tone.

"Kinston, please don't lie to me," she begged. "I know that you're not at the end or even in the middle of a divorce proceeding." Kinston was silent. "Why didn't you tell me?"

"Babe, I didn't know how," he said lowly. "I didn't want to hurt you—"

"You didn't want to hurt me?" Charvette fired, cutting him off. "You don't think it hurt me to find out on my own?"

Kinston didn't ask how she was so certain he and Naomi were an actively married couple. He thought it best to leave well enough alone for the moment.

"I'm sorry, Vette." He attempted to hold her more tightly in an effort to ease her pain and, at the same time, satisfy his growing sexual urge. "I should have told you."

"Yeah, you should have!" she said almost yelling. "You could have at least given me the choice of whether or not I wanted to continue seeing you. But here I am thinking that you are practically single and you are going home every night to Naomi, or lying to her about where you are when you're with me!"

"Baby, I . . ."

"I told you when I met you, Kinston, that I did not date married men, and you claimed you had nothing to hide."

"We're not even really back together," he attempted.

"Then why is she at your house! Opening your

front door, living there! Telling people that it's her and her husband's house!"

"You've been to my house?" Kinston pulled away and sat up to lean against the headboard, alarmed.

"I've been to your house plenty of times! As a matter of fact, you're the one who took me there."

"Baby, you know Naomi doesn't live there. She on that 'call things that's not like you want them to be,' or some mess she done got from church. As far as her telling people she lives there, I don't know what you're talking about. And how would you know that anyway?" he questioned, becoming angry.

"You know exactly what I'm talking about, Kinston," she fired, ignoring his question. "You've been telling me that you've had to work late and all that other bull when really you and Naomi have patched things up! And I'm angry that instead of telling me and letting me decide whether I wanted to continue seeing you, you played me, Kinston! You took me for a fool!" Proverbial daggers shot from her eyes as she glared at Kinston. "You know what? You need to get out of my house." Kinston didn't move but sat pensively still as he bit into his lower lip. "Get up, get your clothes, and get out!" she spat, snatching the covers from the bed and stomping to her bathroom in tears.

She locked the door behind her and stood silent at the sink watching a steady stream of tears flow from her eyes and listening for movement on the other side of the door. A few minutes passed before she heard Kinston rustling about.

"Charvette, can you come out so I can at least say good-bye?" Kinston asked, holding a phone book in his hand with the intention of slapping her in the face with it for having the audacity to come to his home unannounced. Charvette didn't respond. "Vette, please come out here. I promise I'll leave. I just want to hold you one more time," he pleaded. He thought about just kicking the door in but then thought better of it, not wanting to leave any evidence of an altercation just in case she'd be brave enough to call the police. He stood outside the bathroom studying the pattern in the carpet for a full three minutes before placing the phone book back where he'd gotten it and seeing himself out.

After two more minutes had passed, and not fully certain that he was gone, Charvette cracked the door and listened for stirring or any other sound before she exited, dragging the queen-sized comforter behind her. She took a seat on her bed and picked up a photo of her and Kinston that they'd taken in New York. Kinston stood behind her with his arms draped around her shoulders and his lips pressed against her cheek. Charvette had a wide smile spread across her face while her hands hung on Kinston's arms. "I can't believe I trusted that fool," she muttered. She wanted to remove the photo from its frame and tear it up but didn't have the strength. Instead, she placed it in the nightstand drawer and slammed it shut.

Not even forty-eight hours went before Kinston, forgetting his previous rage, had worked his way into Charvette's bed and into her body again.

Now staring up at the ceiling feeling ashamed and hurt, she whispered in her head, *Last time, last time,* as Kinston rolled away and drifted off to sleep.

On the Road Again

"You all ready to go?" Rossi asked as he pulled his Ray-Bans from his face and glanced around the small foyer for Micah's bag. Excited that she would finally meet Rossi's mother, and feeling mounting anticipation of receiving a ring, she smiled as she pecked his lips.

"Yep, just let me grab my keys."

"You sure you ready to meet the family?" he asked, raising the handle to her Pullman, then tilting it toward him to roll it outside.

"They're cooking, right?" she joked. "Because if you get me all the way to Georgia and ain't nobody cooked a good southern meal, I'ma be mad as a dog."

"Well, you don't have anything to worry about. Between my mom and aunt cooking up everything under the sun, you will probably gain about ten pounds this weekend." He slapped her behind before striding toward the door. "With your sexy self."

Micah pulled her Coach shades from atop her

head, then slid them onto her face, picked up her laptop, and followed Rossi out the door. In a matter of minutes, they both were settled into the front seats of Rossi's Expedition and headed for 95 South. With her computer positioned in her lap, Micah opened her e-mail package to review the messages she'd downloaded right before Rossi arrived. She planned to save any messages requiring her response to "drafts" and would send them as soon as she was in a position to get online again.

She responded to a few time-off requests, plotting dates on her calendar, and sent general responses to other messages requiring her attention. The next message was from Jules Turnberry and marked urgent.

> Micah,
> I am so very sorry to have to deliver this message via e-mail; I attempted calling you several times to no avail.
> I have received a sexual harassment complaint from one of your direct reports. As you know, the company has a no-tolerance policy against any acts of harassment shown toward any employee. While these allegations have not be proven, and thus you are not being accused of anything today, unfortunately, corporate policy states that effective upon receipt of the complaint, the accused must be suspended without pay until a full investigation is completed.
> I am not sure at this point how long the investigation will take, but you can anticipate not reporting to work for the next several weeks. During this time, you may call our

corporate HR offices, located in Denver,
Colorado, with any questions you may have.
Again, I am very sorry to have to deliver this
news in this manner. Attached is a copy of the
letter we received from Anthony McDonald
detailing his complaint.

In horror, Micah clicked on the attachment to
launch the Word document.

Mr. Turnberry,
This is a letter requesting the help of
Human Resources in dealing with a
situation where I am being sexually
harassed on a daily and continual basis by
my manager, Micah Abraham. Her constant
sexual innuendos and subtle yet
inappropriate requests for sexual favors are
very detrimental to both the quality of my
work life and my home life. I am desperately
seeking your, or anybody on the HR staff's,
assistance by mediating on my behalf or by
taking action to stop the harassing
behavior. I have included below some
examples of Ms. Abraham's lewd behavior.
Ms. Abraham constantly makes inappropriate
and suggestive comments that upset me to
the degree that I cannot fully focus on
increasing my team's performance. Because
of this, my team has missed sales goals
month over month, for which Ms. Abraham
has written me up.
While I am eating lunch she has made
comments like, "You are licking that ice cream
like you know what you are doing," and "If you
enjoy a tasty meal, I've got a little something

you can snack on."

When I am at my desk working, she has often sneaked up behind me to massage my shoulders, many times letting her hands travel down to my chest.

Back in April, she hinted that I would not have to worry about my team achieving our sales goals if I would have a nightcap with her. She said that she could easily inflate my team's stats and line me up for bonuses and awards, but that the ball was in my court. As she said this, she glanced down at my crotch, letting her eyes linger as she made emphasis on the word "ball."

When Timothy Gaines resigned from his position last month, she asked me if I would be interested in having the Supervisor II position, then added, "You know what you gotta do to get it, right?" before I could give a response.

She has also asked me a few times if my wife is "doing me right at home."

All of these things make it very uncomfortable for me to work with her and for her. I am very miserable in my current role, but I feel like I am in a catch-22, because I cannot afford to quit my job. I am very much a family man, with three children at home who look to me for food and shelter. At the same time, I nearly hate my job because of what I have to deal with on a daily basis with Ms. Abraham.

Once Ms. Abraham's behavior became more consistent, like every week, I did express to her that I did not appreciate her comments, and that they made me

uncomfortable and that I needed for her to respect me as well as my marital
relationship. She only laughed and walked
away after she said as long as I wasn't
making my sales numbers, she could say
anything she wanted to.
As I said before, I am so angry and frustrated
that I can't concentrate on what I am
supposed to be doing when I come to work
each day. And I really hope that something
can be done about her without me losing my
job.
I sincerely hope that my claim is taken
seriously and that one or more of the
following actions will take place:

- I would like to have her officially reprimanded
  and instructed to stop.
- I would like to be removed from under her
  leadership.
- I would like to have her told to stay away
  from me with severe ramifications if she
  violates that instruction.

Honestly, I think she is dangerous to the liveli-
hood of all male employees and I feel that she
should be fired.
Thank you for your help in this matter. You can
reach me at 555-9457 (home phone) or 555-
0456 (cell phone). Please call me after work
hours, as I do not want my manager and fellow
workers to know that I am filing a complaint.
Sincerely,
J. Anthony McDonald
As Micah read, she couldn't control the tears,

spawned by Anthony's lies, that formed in her eyes and began to flow down her face.

"What's wrong, babe?" Rossi crinkled his brows after noting Micah's hand clasped over her mouth and her tear-streaked face.

"That dog!" she spat, reaching up to rub her temples, suddenly plagued by a headache. "I can't believe this fool," she muttered between gasps. A single hand moved from the side of her head to the bridge of her nose, then began to massage there, causing her shades to rise and fall until they finally tumbled toward her lap and down between her seat and the door.

"What is it, sweetie?" Rossi kept his eyes on the road, though concerned with what had Micah in tears.

"This man has gone and filed a sexual harassment complaint against me," she said, holding her head in her palms.

"Who, Micah?"

"Anthony McDonald," she answered, then cleared her throat before she continued in a shaky voice. "I just read an e-mail from Jules Turnberry in HR saying that he filed a sexual harassment charge against me."

Rossi was silent for a few seconds, keeping his focus on the highway while Micah's words rolled around in his head. Though less than half a minute passed, it seemed like an eternity to Micah, making her perplexed about his lack of response.

"Did you hear what I just said?" Micah's exasperation was evident.

"I heard you. Calm down! I'm just thinking," he snapped back. The silence lingered for a few more seconds before he spoke again. "Why would he do something like that, Micah?"

"Because he's pissed that I wrote him up not too long ago!" she exclaimed as her hands flew upward, then landed on her keyboard.

"You said you were talking to him in the club the other night. Have you flirted with him at all?" Rossi questioned in an even tone.

"What?" Micah said near screaming. "What the hell do you mean by that?!"

"I'm just asking. Think about your interaction with him. Have you done anything that could be remotely questionable?" Micah stared at Rossi incredulously, trying to make some sense of what he seemed to be insinuating. "I mean, I'm just asking because you know how touchy-feely you are."

Tilting her head back, Micah stared at a spot directly above her. What had started as a little temple pain had emerged into a full-blown migraine. Stunned by Rossi's lack of compassion and what sounded to her like an accusation, she kept silent as hot, furious tears trickled from the outside corners of her eyes into her ears. *Is this the same man who grabbed a gun and ran to my defense just a few nights ago?* she thought. *It can't be!* Every curse word that she knew, and some that she'd just made up, rolled through her head, although she kept them all to herself.

Ten minutes passed with no conversation between the couple and Tank blaring from the speakers.

"Well?" Rossi questioned.

"Rossi, don't talk to me right now."

"Why not? I'm just asking some questions. You are gonna have to go through this if they do an investigation," he reasoned. "So you might as well prepare yourself. Why can't you answer the question,

Micah? What is it that you are doing to this man to make him come after you like this?"

"To be honest, Rossi, I thought I would get some support from you, not an interrogation!" Micah spat. "Now here I am with my job at risk, and all you can fix your mouth to say to me is 'you know how touchy-feely you are,'" she mocked. "You make me sick!" she ended, slamming her hand against the dash.

"I don't know what you're getting sick about. I'm just asking you some questions."

"What about saying, 'Baby, it's going to be all right. Honey, I'm here to support you. I know you didn't do anything like that. Sweetie, it's all going to work out fine.'? How about saying something like that, Rossi?!"

"I mean were you letting him hit the bootie or something, then all of a sudden took it back, so now he's sabotaging you? Then you got me in the streets looking for him." Micah stared at Rossi in complete disbelief. "I mean, what's really going on here, Micah? Here I am about to marry you and it sound's like you've got a few skeletons popping out of your closet," he added.

"You know what? Just stop the damn truck!" she demanded, then paused for a few seconds furious enough to get out on I-95. "Pull over right now!"

As if she'd said nothing at all, Rossi ignored her ranting. "You sound ridiculous," he said nonchalantly.

"Let me out of this truck, Rossi!" she continued as she slid her laptop in her bag and pulled her purse up on her shoulder. "If that is the best you can do in supporting me, I don't want nothing to do with you. I don't want to go anywhere with you, be with you, I don't even want to see your face!"

she shrieked as angry tears began to flow down her cheeks.

Rossi drove another hour and a half before traffic slowed to a barely moving ten miles an hour just across the Virginia/North Carolina state line. Still fuming, Micah unexpectedly yanked her door open and attempted to hop out of the truck, not caring that she was miles away from home. She pushed off the seat, but before she could land her feet on the pavement, which moved beneath her much more quickly than she had anticipated, Rossi quickly wrapped his right arm around her shoulder and tried to pull her toward him.

"What the hell are you doing!" he barked, jamming on his brakes, battling to maintain control of the vehicle and doing his best to yank Micah back inside. "Get in the truck, Micah, before you make me wreck!"

"Let go of me!" Micah struggled to get out of his grasp, but with her feet sticking straight out from the open door, she could hardly gain enough leverage to free herself.

"Stop acting like a fool!" Rossi pulled over to the shoulder to get them both out of harm's way but held firmly to Micah as the vehicle rolled to a stop. Then he shifted into park with his left hand. "What the hell is wrong with you?!" he yelled, finally letting her go.

In an instant Micah jumped out of the truck and began walking in the opposite direction just as a State Police Officer eased his cruiser behind them. Not slowing her stride for a second, Micah continued to stomp as she dialed Erin's number.

"Girl, I'm going to need you to come get me," she huffed once Erin picked up. She glanced over her shoulder for a split second to see the officer approaching the driver's side of Rossi's truck.

"Come get you from where? I thought you were on the road headed for Georgia."

"I was, but, girl, Rossi has gotten on my last nerve. Ouch!" she wailed as she inadvertently kicked up a rock between her flip-flop and the sole of her foot.

"Where are you?" Erin asked, confused.

"Out here on the interstate. I jumped out of the truck."

"What? Where's Rossi?"

"Back there talking to the State Trooper." Just as she finished her sentence, she saw another cruiser slowing its pace as it approached her. "Can you come get me?"

"Where on the interstate are you, Micah?"

"Ma'am, is there a problem? What's going on out here?" the officer questioned the moment he stepped foot out of his car.

"There's no problem," Micah shot back as she glanced at the last name "Mayo" pinned to his uniform, then replied to Erin, "We just crossed the state line."

"Okay, that's like two or three hours away!"

"Ma'am, I need you to get off the phone and help me understand this situation," Officer Mayo calmly but firmly stated.

"I'll call you back," Micah spoke into the phone before closing it. "It's really nothing. We just had a little disagreement; that's all," she said, folding her arms across her chest. "And I don't want to go anywhere with him." In her peripheral vision she saw the other officer approaching from several feet away. "I'm just going to have someone pick me up."

"What were the two of you arguing about, if I may ask?" Officer Mayo questioned.

"He's just stupid," she huffed.

"Did he hit you, ma'am?" he asked, with crinkled brows.

"No, he did not."

"Just stay right there for a few minutes, ma'am," he instructed as he turned to his peer. They mumbled words between each other for a few minutes, while Rossi stood leaning on the back of his truck and Micah stood mad as a hornet, shifting her laptop bag over to her other shoulder. Three more minutes passed before the two officers separated to speak individually to both Micah and Rossi.

"Ma'am, we can't allow you to just walk out here on the highway. It's highly dangerous. What I can do is take you to the station and you and your fiancé can work it out there and leave together, if he chooses to follow me there, or you can have someone pick you up from there."

"Okay, that's fine," Micah replied as calmly as she could as she stepped toward the cruiser. Officer Mayo let her in the backseat, exchanged words with his peer, then got in his vehicle and pulled off. Micah looked out of the back window and watched as Rossi pulled behind the cruiser and followed them to the station.

Once there, they were allowed to interact. By this time, Micah had calmed herself enough to act rationally and sensibly, although her face clearly expressed irritation. Rossi carefully approached.

"Baby, you know I love you. You know that." He reached for her hand. She started to snatch it away but thought better of it, remembering where they were. "Can we please get in the car and go?" he

said more as a statement than a question. Micah
did all she could to avoid looking Rossi directly in
his eyes. "Micah, look at me," he coaxed.

When Micah refused, his eyes darted nervously
around the station as he tried to think of what
he could say to get himself out of there as quickly
as possible. Being a black man in the company of
primarily white officers, he just didn't feel safe.
Just the thought of being thrown in a cell for no
good reason was enough to make his insides flip,
and it wasn't quite what he had in mind for the
weekend.

"Baby, maybe I didn't say the right thing, but
please believe me when I tell you that I love you.
You're the queen of my soul, Micah. I wish you
would come on with me and let's get out of here."

"Why would I want to go anywhere with you,
Rossi? Why?" she expressed with her hands as well
as her mouth. "You practically agreed with this id-
iotic false claim against me and . . ."

"Baby, lower your voice," he firmly instructed,
then paused with lifted brows. "I did not accuse
you of anything. I know you don't believe me,
but I am always in your corner. I didn't approach
the situation right, and I'm sorry for that. I
should have been more careful and sensitive to
the situation, but I dropped the ball. I'm sorry,"
he said nearly pleading with deep furrows across
his forehead. "Now I hope you can find it in your
heart to forgive me and move on with me. I don't
want to leave you here." There was a pensive
pause before he continued. "If you are going to
be my wife, we are going to have disagreements
sometimes, and I don't want to think that every
time something comes up you're going to want
to run from the problem."

"I'm not running from the problem; I'm running from you," she chided.

"So are you gonna run from me once we get married? Is this what I'm going to have to deal with every time you get mad?" He stopped long enough to allow her to answer but continued after a few seconds. "Well, is it? Because, baby, I'm gonna make some mistakes. If I can't promise you anything else, I can guarantee you that I'm not always going to get it right . . . and neither are you." Micah kept silent while she stared into Rossi's eyes. She was too angry to admit with her lips that he was right, but Rossi felt a coming sense of relief, as he could detect her softening. "Now I'm committed to you and our relationship, which means working through our issues, not dropping the relationship at the first sign of trouble." Lifting her hand, he moved in for his closing argument. "I'm excited about my family being able to meet you, which they are expecting to do tonight and tomorrow, so I'm going to say it one more time: Please, let's leave—together—and we can work out the rest away from here."

With a defeated sigh, Micah dug in her purse and called Erin back. "Hey. . . . No, I'm all right. You don't have to come get me. . . . Yeah. . . . I'll call you later. . . . All right, bye." She then moved to lift her bag, but Rossi grabbed it for her.

"I've got it, babe. Let's go."

Rossi took quick steps over to Officer Mayo to make sure there were no issues with the two of them leaving.

"So everything is okay with you two?" he asked.

"We're fine," Rossi mumbled and nodded, then motioned for Micah to join him and gingerly took her hand into his own when she approached.

"Well, be safe, and, ma'am, no more attempted leaps from moving vehicles for you. You were lucky he held on to you the way he did," Officer Mayo reprimanded. "I know plenty of men who would have let their woman jump and kept going."

Embarrassed, Micah smirked and responded with "Yes, sir," as she tugged at the hem of her T-shirt to lay it neatly across the waistline of her jeans.

"Thank you, sir," Rossi concluded, reaching for the officer's hand for a shake, letting his free arm circle Micah's waist.

"Glad I could help."

At that the couple headed for the door in peace. Once they had gotten back inside the truck and had pulled out of the lot, Rossi chuckled as he shook his head. "I can't believe you. You 'bout to have me locked up over some foolishness."

"Whatever," Micah mumbled, reclining her seat and closing her eyes. "Wake me up when we get there."

Opportunity Knocks

Micah attempted to make the best of the time off from work and search for another job. "Always have a plan B," she said out loud as she settled on her couch with a cup of tea, her laptop, and her cell phone. A few minutes into her searching, her phone rang. Recognizing Victori's number, she answered right away.

"What are you doing today?" Victori asked. "I thought you might be free to have lunch since you have a few days off."

"Right now, I'm looking for another job, just in case things get worse before they get better," she answered pessimistically.

"Do you really think it's going to come to that?"

"I have no idea what it's going to come to, but I need to be prepared for anything. If you had told me last month that I'd be sitting here on suspension right now, I never would have believed it. And to be honest with you, the allegations are so unfounded I thought I'd only be out a few days, but it's turned into two whole weeks."

"How much longer do you think it will be?"

"I have no idea, but what I do know is I can't afford to be without a job right now."

"Well you have Rossi. I'm sure he will help you out if you get in a bind."

"Girl, I can't depend on him," Micah huffed as she rolled her eyes. "Let me tell you what he said after I told him about this so-called investigation." Micah spent the next few minutes sharing with her friend what had taken place on the ride to Georgia and how she had felt totally unsupported by Rossi. "After we left the police station, we didn't talk about it anymore."

"Rossi gets on my last nerve. I know you love him and all that, but, girl, I couldn't put up with that mess. Here you are at risk of losing your job and that is the best thing he could say out of his mouth."

"That wasn't even the worst part of the trip," Micah continued, still feeling embarrassed about what she was about to share.

"Okay . . . ?" Victori asked in a questioned pause.

Micah sighed first, then spoke. "Girl, we get to the family reunion, right, and everybody's walking around having a good-old time eating and whatnot. He takes my video camera and starts going around to his family members, laughing, talking to them, playing around and all that. Girl, this Negro goes to every single person there except me."

"How did he leave you out?"

"I don't know. I'm still trying to figure that out. But wait a minute, there's more. Girl, his sister tries to introduce me to his mom and aunts and says, 'This is Micah, Rossi's girlfriend.' Then Rossi gets really offended and blurts out, 'Romni, can I have some business please? Why do you feel the need to share that? Did anybody ask you to make introductions for me?"

"Oh no he didn't!"

"Oh yes he did. Then to add to that, his aunt says, 'Well, who is she then?' Rossi was completely silent. He didn't say one word."

Erin gasped in disbelief. "He didn't say *anything?*"

"Not one single word, girl; just stood there looking stupid and on the spot. Then he walked off talking about he was going to go get a hot dog, and left me standing there."

"Oh my goodness," Victori expressed, shaking her head. "Girl, please leave that man alone. He don't want you 'cause ain't no man in his right mind gonna sit up there and do something like that."

"Rossi left me standing right there feeling like I had hitchhiked my way to his family reunion. I was so embarrassed and humiliated I didn't know what to do."

"So what *did* you do?"

"What could I do but stand there, look stupid, and wish I had driven my own car? And believe me, if I had, I would have been on my way back home at that very moment."

"So he never introduced you as his fiancée?"

"Not his fiancée, not his girlfriend, not nothing. Like I said, it was just like he picked me up from the side of the road and I just happened to be going to the exact same place."

"Micah, I don't mean to sound crude, but how can you even think of marrying a man like that? A man who won't even acknowledge you in front of his family. I mean, is he going to invite them to the wedding?"

"Don't beat me up about it, Victori," Micah sighed.

"I'm not beating you up, but I'm just saying, you deserve so much more than that." The octave of Victori's voice began to change, rising higher as she expressed her anger. "Here you are, beautiful, professional, got something going for you, and you'd be a prize for any man. And he's going to carry you like that? Pffff! Girl, he couldn't do me like that. I woulda beat his ass right there in front of his momma, cousins, aunts, uncles, brothers, *and* sisters!"

"Girl, I was so shocked I couldn't even think straight."

"Yeah, and I see why, but I would have thought enough to go upside his head with a pack of hamburger rolls or something! I would have turned that park upside down, and from that day on, his family would have been like, 'Well, that might not be his girlfriend, but she shole did whup his ass out here'!"

The two ladies laughed before Micah refocused on her task. "Girl, let me get back to what I was doing. I need to make good use of my time, plus I don't want to get depressed all over again thinking about it."

"All right, girl. Well, call me later if you get a break in your day, and let me know if you want me to go round Rossi's house and smack him up a little bit," Victori joked, although she knew that Micah was hurting inside.

"I might be free in a couple of hours, and I could use a little girlfriend time. I'll give you a call back," she ended.

An hour later, she'd found a few positions that caught her interest, and with a few clicks of her mouse, she'd shot off her résumé to each company. Feeling a sense of accomplishment, she rose to her feet, stretched momentarily, then shuffled to her bathroom to start the shower, thinking about the conversation she'd had with Victori.

As the water warmed, she picked up the phone and dialed Victori's number. "Hey, can you check and see what the rest of the crew is doing?" she started, referring to Charvette and Erin. "Let's try to go to brunch. You know I need a few shoulders to cry on," she said, semichuckling.

"Cool, let me give them a ring and I'll call you back."

"I'll be in the shower, so if I don't answer just leave me a message." At that, Micah ended the call, undressed, and stepped into the warm spray of water. Leaning her head back, she shampooed her tresses, planning to massage in some mousse and let her locks air-dry into shiny tendrils. She lathered her body with a soapy loofah while trying to figure out what she had done to deserve her recent string of not so good luck.

"Well, it's Sunday morning, and you should have your butt in church, instead of here at home with your laptop and trying to go out with your girls," she mumbled to herself. As a matter of fact, now that she thought about it, she couldn't remember the last time she'd crossed the threshold of a place of worship. "I gotta do better," she said as she rinsed the suds from her body, then stepped out of the tub.

On her way to the closet, she heard the chiming of her cell phone, indicating a missed call. Thinking it was Victori who'd called, she rushed toward it and flipped it open only to see that the missed call was from Rossi. Rolling her eyes, she tossed the phone onto her bed, then padded to the closet for a pair of jeans and a T-shirt, but then thought better of her choice. Instead, she selected a light chiffon Japanese floral print dress in white, yellow, and blue featuring a double V-neck that revealed enough skin to give her a little sex appeal and an empire waist that added a breezy feel. She picked a pair of heeled sandals that wrapped at the ankle and dug through a box of jewelry and found a few matching pieces.

Once she was dressed, she admired her appearance in the full-length mirror, then smiled at herself. "I do deserve better," she commented aloud. "And today I'm going to treat myself."

It wasn't until she began applying a little makeup that she realized she'd not yet heard back from Victori, but she shrugged it off, deciding to have lunch out even if she had to do it alone. Just as she grabbed her keys Victori rang back.

"Where are we eating?" Micah chirped upon answering.

"Let's go to that little spot down on Park Avenue."

"Cool. I'm on my way out the door right now," Micah said, taking hold of her purse and reaching for the knob on the front door. "Is everybody coming?"

"Yep. Lucky for you, everyone was free this morning."

"That's 'cause we're all a bunch of heathens. I'll see you in a few," she said, ending the call.

Waking Up to Reality

"So you mean to tell me that you went all the way to Savannah, Georgia, and his trifling, selfish butt didn't even tell his family that you are his fiancée?!" Charvette nearly shouted across the table.

"Just let everybody know, why don't you," Micah spoke over her menu as the ladies sat crammed in a booth at *Kuba Kuba,* a mom-and-pop Cuban restaurant.

"I'm just saying, though," she continued, lowering her voice a bit, "why he take you all the way down there if he won't gonna make an announcement?"

Micah shrugged as she read the menu description for a tortilla con chorizo. "This sounds good," she said, regretting that she'd even brought the subject up. "An omelet with Spanish sausage, potatoes, green peppers, and onions." The ladies completely ignored her attempted diversion.

"So he didn't say anything? He had to say something," Erin pressed. "I mean, he had to give some kind of response."

"I just told y'all he didn't crack his lips! He went and got a hamburger or something. I don't even remember." Micah waved her hand in dismissal, trying to pretend that it hadn't bothered her much, but her friends could tell that she was both hurt and embarrassed by the incident.

"So he left you standing there looking stupid?" Charvette said more as a statement than a question. She blew into her cup of black coffee, then rolled her eyes before taking a sip.

"Pretty much. Can we change the subject now?"

"And you still gonna marry his ass?" Victori balked incredulously. "You's a better woman than me," she added, slapping her menu on the table. "What's his phone number, 'cause I'm about to call him and cuss his ass out!"

"All right y'all, all right," Micah uttered as her eyes began to water. "I don't wanna talk about it anymore." The table was silent for a few seconds. "Erin, let me out please. I'm going to the ladies' room. Order me this right here," she said, pointing to her meal choice then sliding out of the booth once Erin stood. She tipped across the small diner on her stilettos and disappeared behind the restroom door.

"Hmph! She stupid," Victori blurted.

"You need to cut it out and stop being so judgmental," Erin shot.

"Well, she is being stupid," Victori exclaimed. "Running behind Rossi like he's the last chicken to be fried. Well, I got news for her—grocery stores sell chicken every day."

"So what do you have to say about somebody like yourself who stays in the store picking up bird after doggone bird?" Charvette asked, referring to

Victori's promiscuous track record. "You act like you just can't live without a man."

"Don't hate on my sexiness," Victori replied, with a smirk, as she used her hands to plump her semiexposed bosom.

"If you were half as sexy as you think you are, you wouldn't be jumping from man to man, regardless if he's someone else's or not," Erin blurted before waving their server over.

Victori grappled for her next words, but none came to mind, so she sat with her mouth and eyes stretched wide open until the waitress appeared to take their orders. As she finished, Micah reappeared.

"What'd I miss, ladies?"

Victori opened her mouth, but Erin cut her off before she could get started. "Nothing. Shut up, Victori."

"Micah, Rossi just doesn't deserve you," Charvette asserted. "He takes you for granted and you are worth so much more."

"You know what?" Micah started. "I thought when I left the table I said I didn't want to talk about this anymore. I know you all made your comments while I was gone, and I stayed a few extra minutes to let you get it all out of your system. I come back, and the conversation is still focused on me. And since you all have chosen to continue to harp on me, let me say a few things, and don't anybody take offense." Micah was silent for two seconds as she pressed her lips tightly together. "Victori, until you stop sleeping with every Ronnie, Bobby, Ricky, and Mike you can't judge me. I'd like to call a spade a spade, but I respect our friendship too much. Charvette, until you realize that you don't deserve to be the other woman, there is not much you can say to me in terms of relationship advice. And Erin, I don't recall any successful relationships popping off on your end. I can only remember three miserably failed ones in the last four years. What that suggests to me is that all of us have a few lessons to learn. So," she paused once more, "I don't want to hear another word about it. Okay?" She pasted a phony smile on her face and looked in each of her friend's eyes.

"Touché," Charvette replied coolly. "And just for the record, I'm not seeing Kinston anymore," she announced.

"Since when? The day before yesterday?" Victori laughed.

"You're so funny," Charvette sneered. "Let's just eat," she finished as the server brought over platters carefully balanced on both arms.

The ladies dug into their meals silently, giving Micah more time to think about what her friends had expressed. She knew they called themselves looking out for her best interest, but sometimes Micah didn't want their feedback; what she really wanted was a listening ear or two. The commentary was just unnecessary. And she had thought the incident over at least fifty times in her head and could come up with no reasonable explanation for why Rossi hadn't introduced her as his fiancée, especially when asked. *Maybe he doesn't really love me. He can't. Love doesn't manifest itself this way, does it?* she questioned herself.

In her heart she knew her girls were right; she didn't deserve the treatment she received from

Rossi. Micah knew that she'd have to find the strength from somewhere to let Rossi go.

The only noise at their table was the sound of forks clanking against the glass plates, as the women seemed to be afraid to broach any subject until one of Victori's microbraids fell out from her head and onto the table. Suddenly the group burst into laughter.

"Somebody kill that spider!" Charvette squealed.

"Girl, I told you about getting your hair done at Ray-Ray and them house," Erin added.

"And I keep telling you that I'm open to donations if you want me to go to the African lady. Can I taste your omelet?" she said, ready to stab her fork into Erin's plate.

Erin quickly drew her plate back before Victori's fork made contact. "Uh-uh, girl! I'll cut you a piece. That fork been in your mouth and I don't know what was in your mouth before that." The table burst into laughter again while Victori rolled her eyes. "Don't be offended; you know it's the truth."

"Anyway . . ." Victori dismissed, caught up in a giggle herself. "So what's up with that fine brother from the club? He single?" she directed to Micah.

"You know what? I really don't know because I haven't talked to him," she responded, then filled her mouth with food.

"Well, give me his number," Charvette injected. "I'll call him . . . if he's single, that is," she added, making reference to Micah's remark. "How did you end up with his card again? I know you didn't take it out his hand, because you act like the only man left alive in the whole wide world is Rossi Evans." She rolled her eyes as she spoke.

"I told you, he must have stuck it on my car that night we went out," Micah said, referring to Stephen's magnetic card. He had strategically attached it as she pulled off in front of him at the club weeks ago. It wasn't until two days later that Micah took note of it. Quickly Micah nudged Erin under the table. "Speak of the devil. . . ." She nodded her head toward the entrance, causing all three ladies to swivel like bar stools toward the door.

"What?! Who?!" Victori screeched.

"Deg y'all! Learn how to be discreet," Micah chastised.

Erin and Charvette turned their heads back to their plates just as fast as they'd looked at the door, but Victori's head bobbed and weaved like a boxer's as she strained to see Stephen come in. Erin kicked Victori beneath the table.

"Girl, turn around!" she barked over Victori's yelp in pain.

In a matter of seconds, Stephen had spotted Micah and begun his short stroll over to the ladies' table.

"Good morning," he said respectfully, with a charming smile, as he looked directly at Micah. His hair was neatly edged with sharp lines that bordered his locks, his skin looked smooth and polished, and his teeth gleamed radiantly. "How are you ladies doing?" Right away Charvette glanced at his hand in search of a ring, Victori's line of vision beelined to his crotch, and Erin pretended to be engrossed in her meal, but Micah found herself momentarily caught in the captivating look in his warm eyes. Before she realized it, a smile had crept across her face.

"Just fine, thank you," Micah answered graciously. "How about yourself?"

"Wonderful now that I've run into you a second time." Micah couldn't help but blush as her friends chortled a little louder than she would have allowed if she could control them. Erin poked into her thigh with one hand while she lifted her drink to her lips. There were a few seconds of awkward silence before Stephen spoke again. "So how is your"—he paused to scan the half-eaten food on the platters in front of the women, taking note of eggs, sausage, and breakfast potatoes—"breakfast, I take it?"

"It's pretty good," Victori started. "Let me ask you a question: are you married?" she asked shamelessly.

"No, I'm not," Stephen responded without hesitation. "If I were, I'd be at home cooking my wife breakfast and serving it to her in bed, instead of running in here to pick up something for just myself," he stated coolly, letting his gaze float back over to Micah, where it rested briefly. "So I have to ask you ladies the same. Are you married?" he asked, looking at each of them, but interested in only Micah's response.

"No, but Micah's engaged," Victori shot out, pointing to Micah and earning another kick to her shin. "Oww!"

"Is that right?" Stephen asked, with a single raised brow. "Where's your ring?" he inquired.

Micah instantly felt heat rising in her face as she jammed her hand under the table and onto her lap. "I . . . umm . . . it's being . . ."

Stephen didn't let her finish, immediately discerning that there was no ring to speak of. "Don't answer that," he said, resting a hand on her shoulder. "It's none of my business. I shouldn't even have asked," he ended. "You ladies go ahead and enjoy your meals. I hope to see you again soon . . . Micah."

Stephen smiled as he walked toward the bar to pick up his take-out order, pleased that Micah's finger was bare. In his mind, no ring meant no engagement, which meant Micah was available.

New Places,
New Faces

Romni stuffed another load of laundry into Rossi's washing machine, then unpacked her last box of personal items and put them neatly away. Although she didn't have two dollars to her name, she felt good just being able to relax without the fear of T-Dog bursting in consumed with anger and using her for a punching bag.

As planned, Romni had quit her job in Savannah and transitioned away from all that she was familiar with in an effort to begin her life again. T-Dog hadn't wanted to let her go, but he simply didn't have a choice. Initially when she'd announced that she'd be moving to Virginia, his reaction had been the same as it had always been when he was angry, which was to hit her, because he thought it would force her into submission, just as it had in times past.

"The more you hit me, the more determined I am to leave your ass!" she'd cried out after he'd slammed her into a wall. "And then whatchu gone do?"

"You ain't going no got-damn where without me! 'Cause I'm a rollin' stone, baby. Wherever you lay your ass is my home. You best believe that," he'd replied assuredly.

From that day, Romni never mentioned her leaving again, knowing that if she wanted to escape with her life and no further bruises and injuries she had to keep her mouth shut. For three solid weeks she did whatever it took to keep peace in her home besides engaging in sex. She said nothing about T-Dog spending more and more time at Crystal's apartment, and she served his meals as she had always done but not before letting the flies get first dibs. Knowing that T-Dog's body was becoming more and more contaminated, she found it increasingly difficult to even sleep in the same bed as T-Dog. She did what she could to work late hours to encourage him to seek sexual fulfillment elsewhere, and fortunately for her, her strategies worked. Not soon enough the Evans family reunion was held, and when Rossi hit the road to head back home, Romni climbed in the back of his truck and waved good-bye to her past.

Now as she lay on her stomach centered on the full-sized guest bed at her brother's house with a pad of paper and pen, she thought about what her next steps should be. Finding a job topped the list. Next she listed writing a letter to her mother to let her know she was happy and free. She could just as easily have picked up the phone and called Josephine, but her mother had a way of taking over the conversation and Romni was sure she wouldn't be able to express herself like she wanted to. Other than that, Romni couldn't think of much else. She planned to spend her free time in prayer, reading God's word, and looking for a good church to attend and join. It had been a long time since she'd put her singing voice to good use, and she could think of no better place to use it than in a church choir.

"Thank you, Lord," she whispered, sliding off the bed and onto her knees. "Thank you for your mercy, grace, and loving kindness."

Charvette sat at her kitchen table with a cup of coffee and a slice of toast beside herself with yearning for Kinston. Her television was tuned to *The Daily Buzz,* a morning personality-infused news program, but paid little attention to the show's hosts. Her thoughts were primarily focused on the man she loved. She couldn't deny that she was indeed angry with his lack of honesty, yet she missed him terribly. It had been several weeks since she'd last seen or talked to him, but not a day went by that she didn't wish for his touch and come close to dialing his number.

Suddenly an idea dropped into her head. Charvette moved quickly to her desktop computer and pulled up a new document on Microsoft Word. In the center of the page in large bold letters she typed three words: *I miss you.* After printing the sheet, she inserted it in an envelope and typed in Kinston's street address but left off his name as well as a return address. If Kinston got the letter, she was pretty sure he would conclude it was from her. And if his wife got the letter, she was pretty sure a heated argument would start over whom the letter was intended for and felt that whatever ramifications Kinston would face would be well deserved.

Without further thought, she headed for her car and drove nearly an hour away to Spotsylvania to drop the letter in the mail, not wanting the Richmond postmark to give her away. Her conscience screamed as she circled her car around the lot to a cluster of mailboxes, but it wasn't strong enough to stop her from extending her arm out of the window and dropping the letter inside. Pulling away, she headed back for Richmond to her shop.

Keep Your
Options Open

"So what exactly are you looking to do?" Stephen questioned as he glanced over the miniprofile Micah had completed while he ended his phone call with another client. He had been elated when he'd received a call from Micah a few days ago with a few housing questions but had hid his excitement beneath his professionalism.

"Well, I'm getting married soon," she started. The truth was she was beginning to seriously contemplate relocating to Charlotte and move on with her life without Rossi. "And, of course, my husband and I plan to live under one roof, so I wanted to look into renting or possibly selling my house."

"Right. I don't think I've ever said congratulations, so congrats," he stated less than genuinely as his eyes instinctively glanced again for a ring but found her finger yet empty.

"I just want to look at what my options are,

because we haven't really decided yet which of our two homes we'll actually live in. We may even purchase a new home altogether. It just depends."

"Okay, so he owns a home too, then."

"Yes, it's a lot older than I'd like it to be, but it's more spacious than my home, so you know, there are pros and cons on both sides," she replied. "We were even thinking about moving to Charlotte, for career reasons and a new start together," she added, thinking he may be able to give her a housing contact in that area when the time came.

"I see." Stephen nodded as he fought to be less mesmerized by Micah's sparkling eyes. "There are definitely some things you can do, and we do offer property management if you'd like to rent it out. If you go with that option, we'd take care of screening your tenants, collecting the rent, and scheduling any maintenance that the property may need. What it does is take some of that landlord pressure off of you. Of course, we send any monies received directly to you within five days, so if you need to continue to make mortgage payments, you will have time to do so," he informed her.

"Hmmm," she pondered. "How much do you think I could rent my place for?"

"Well, let's sit down and talk about what all it has to offer and see if we can work something up. Come on back to my office," he said, turning on his heels and moving down the hallway with Micah following. "So you haven't made a purchasing decision yet?"

"Actually, I can be content with what we have. Like I said, you know, I just want to be aware of what options are available." Micah took a seat in front of Stephen's desk, taking note of the knickknacks and photos. She picked up a five-by-seven frame and smiled at the image of two small children with their heads pressed together beaming brightly at the camera. "They are so cute," she commented.

"Thanks. Those are my nephews." He smiled slightly as he glanced at the photo. "Have you been prequalified yet?" Micah shook her head. Normally Stephen didn't waste his time with customers who had not completed the prequalification process, as that information helped him to determine what properties to show. Nonetheless, he wasn't bothered a bit by it in this instance. His attraction to Micah was worth the half hour she'd be in his office. "Well, let's start by talking about your house. How many bedrooms?"

"Three," she answered quickly.

"Baths?"

"Two and a half."

"Garage?"

Micah shook her head. "Driveway, though," she said, with a smile.

"Fireplace?" he continued, making notes on a legal pad.

"Yes."

"Is it brick?"

"Siding."

"What year was it built?"

"Ninety-two."

"Living room, dining room, den?"

"Yes, yes, and yes. And there's a spacious backyard perfect for a picnic," she replied.

"Would you mind me taking a look at it?"

"Of course not." Micah waved.

"When can we schedule a time?"

"I don't have to be at work for another hour. Now works well for me if you have time."

"Now would be perfect."

As soon as the words tumbled from Stephen's lips, Micah's mind flew to her bedroom. She did make up the bed that morning, but she was certain she'd left a few unmentionables from her bra and panty collection lying about. The rest of the house was in perfect order from the thorough cleaning she'd done the day before.

"Just let me grab an assessment form and we can be on our way." Stephen rose to his feet and took a few steps to a supply closet. He picked up a clipboard and turned toward her. "Ready?"

"Yes. You can follow me in your car," Micah suggested.

"Lead the way."

During the fifteen-minute drive to Micah's house Stephen couldn't help but smile to himself, although Micah was nowhere close to being his. "Gotta start somewhere," he said to himself. He just wasn't sure where to start.

Erin tugged her T-shirt down over the waistline of her khaki capris, then fastened the buckles on her brown, heeled sandals. Before she opened the examining room door, she lay a hand on her belly and twisted her lips, preparing her mind for what Dr. Corbin might say. Coincidentally, it was time for her yearly exam at the same time that her period was late. She smoothed her hand over her hair, opened the door and approached the office door across the hall, and tapped twice.

"Come on in and have a seat," Dr. Corbin called. She glanced up from her desk for just a second to make sure it was Erin who was entering, then began sharing her findings. "Your pregnancy test came back negative.

Erin released a huge sigh. "You just don't know how much weight fell off my shoulders just by hearing you say that," she said, now far less concerned about why her cycle had yet to make its monthly appearance.

"So your weight gain is probably attributed to your eating habits," she stated stoically as she made notes to the patient file in front of her. "Tell me what's going on with that."

With a shrug, Erin admitted, "I could be doing better. I don't think I do too badly, though. I do like to enjoy a good meal."

"There's nothing wrong with enjoying a good meal, but start making some small changes to your diet. Increase your fruit and vegetable intake as well as your water. You want to start doing it now rather than waiting until you get older, when it will be harder to lose weight. After a while you'll start to feel it in your joints and other areas." She lifted her brows, looking almost motherly.

"I do have some concerns, however," Dr. Corbin continued. Right away Erin noticed the change in her gynecologist's voice tone. "Your Pap smear results are abnormal." Dr. Corbin folded her hands and leaned forward on her desk.

Erin rapidly blinked in confusion. "What do you mean?"

"Your test is showing that you've contracted genital human papillomavirus."

"Hu-what?" Erin questioned, feeling her heartbeat pick up its pace.

"Human papillomavirus, or HPV, as it's more commonly known. It's a sexually transmitted disease that fifty percent or more of sexually active men and women acquire at some point in their lives." Erin sat speechless as her eyes began to burn with welling tears that she was able to hold back only until Dr. Corbin spoke her next words. "Many times there are no symptoms, but a person might experience soft pink or flesh-colored warts if it's a low-risk case. In high-risk cases, it can cause cancer of the cervix, vulva, vagina, and/or anus."

"Cancer?" Erin's eyes stretched wide. In her mind cancer meant death.

"Don't panic. I'll have to run some other tests before I can make that diagnosis. Right now you're just showing abnormal Pap smear results."

"Well what do I need to take to clear it up?"

"Unfortunately, there is no 'cure' for HPV infection, although in most women the infection goes away on its own. The treatments provided are directed to the changes in the skin or mucous membrane caused by HPV infection, such as warts and precancerous changes in the cervix. I'm going to have you come back in next week for more tests so we can identify this particular strain. Then you'll need to keep up with your appointments so that we can note any changes or developments." Dr. Corbin pulled three tissues from a box on her desk and handed them to Erin, who wiped at her tears. "Erin, tell me about your sex life. Are you sexually involved with more than one person?"

"No." Erin shook her head. "I've been with the same man and him only for about two years."

"Is the relationship monogamous . . . that you know of?"

"It's supposed to be, but I've had my suspicions, to be honest with you," Erin confessed.

"Are the two of you having protected sex?"

Shaking her head shamefully, Erin looked away. "I guess I call myself trusting him."

"Trust is important in any relationship; however, it is also important to protect the integrity of your health, especially if you have reason to suspect that your partner may be exposing you to other people," Dr. Corbin said in a compassionate reprimand. Erin nodded as she wiped away more tears.

Erin drove home feeling a range of emotions but mostly afraid and bewildered. The words *cancer* and *no cure* repeatedly resounded in her head. *But it can go away on it's own,* she told herself, although it hardly sufficed as encouragement. Paralyzed by fearful thoughts, she was startled when a driver behind her blew his horn when she hadn't moved several seconds after the traffic light turned green. Still dazed, she drove forward, then not quite knowing how she did it, ended up at home.

The next morning came quickly, and from somewhere unbeknownst to her, Erin found the strength to pull herself together and report to work.

"I brought you some breakfast," Erin offered as she stopped at Micah's desk and opened a large flat box of Krispy Kreme doughnuts. She took a seat in a vacant chair and grabbed a doughnut herself. "It's good to have you back," she added, speaking of Micah's return to work. It had been a week since Jules had called to share that not only had Anthony's claim been determined unfounded, but in addition he had quit his job. Micah was allowed to return to work and was compensated with retroactive pay for the time she'd been out.

"Thanks. I'm still trying to catch up on stuff that

fell by the wayside while I was out," Micah replied as she scanned a long list of e-mail messages.

"So are you going to sue Anthony?"

Micah shook her head. "I'm just glad he's out of my hair. I don't ever want to see that man again."

"And I can't blame you, girl." Erin took another bite of her donut before sipping from a coffee cup. "What are you doing this weekend?"

"Probably nothing. The house is squeaky clean since I've had nothing else to do for the past four weeks. And Rossi is working, but even if he weren't, you know we wouldn't be spending time together," Micah replied, rolling her eyes.

"Good, because I need to come over and talk to you."

You've Got Mail

"Charvette's in the hospital," Victori blurted into the phone.

"What happened?" Micah questioned. "Is she okay?"

"I don't know. I'm headed over there now."

"I'll meet you there." Micah pulled away from an Oprah rerun, slid into a pair of flip-flops, and jetted out to her car. In minutes she'd arrived at Bon Secours Richmond Community Hospital and sped down the hallways to find her friend. Running into Erin first, they greeted with a quick hug. "What happened to Charvette?"

"I have no clue. The police were doing a routine drive by her shop and noticed that the door was ajar, although it was dark inside. They said they found her knocked out behind the counter in a very compromising position," Erin shared.

"Where is she now?"

"They have her in emergency surgery."

Micah gasped as they approached Victori, who

was seated in the waiting area. "How long has she been back there?"

"A few hours," Victori stated. "I hope she's all right. I just got off the phone with her dad. He's flying here from California tomorrow."

"Did someone break into the shop or something?" Erin asked, perplexed.

"I doubt it. She has an alarm system that she faithfully sets once the shop closes. It would have gone off if someone had broken in." Victori smeared a tear away. "I don't know what could have happened."

Kinston knocked on the shop's door with a smile on his face, as he'd done in times past. This time he carried no flowers or food, just himself, dressed in a black Nike Core Warm-Up suit and matching tennis shoes. Charvette opened the door slowly, not wanting to seem too anxious, although her heart began beating in triplicate from excitement. Right away he gathered Charvette into his arms and kissed her passionately.

"What are you doing here?" she asked when she could squeeze out a few words.

"I couldn't stay away," he whispered. "I had to see you." His hands roamed her body, touching and squeezing in all the places that he knew would excite her. "I know we can't keep seeing each other, but I had to see you one more time, Vette."

With no defenses built up, Charvette melted at his touch and began unbuttoning her shirt. Kinston dove toward her breasts, peeling back her bra and taking her nipples into her mouth one at a time. Charvette arched her back toward him while a moan escaped her lips. She undid her pants, let them slide to the floor, and stepped out of them. Kinston lifted her half-naked body up onto the receptionist's desk, tugged at the waistband of his pants, fumbled with a lubricated condom, then used his fingers to move her panties to the side and slid inside her. As he started a slow but then increasingly aggressive thrust, Charvette wrapped her legs around his waist and moaned with pleasure.

"I miss you too, baby," Kinston whispered, confirming that he had received her letter. "I miss you so much I had to come see you when I got your letter, but I couldn't get away before now," he said, thrusting forward with more force.

"Kinston," Charvette whispered over and over again. "Baby, don't leave me. I have to have you in my life. I miss you so much."

In another two minutes Kinston reached his release point and let out a deep growl while Charvette kissed all over his chest. Kinston heaved as he withdrew himself from Charvette's body, turned to deposit the condom in a nearby trash can, then spun quickly and punched Charvette in the face. She yelped in both pain and surprise as she fell backward over the desk, hitting her head on a shelf holding various hair products before she landed on the cold, hard tile floor.

"Why are you sending that crap to my house like that?" he bellowed in anger, standing over her. "Here I am trying to patch things up with my wife and you're gonna send that? I don't ever want to see your trifling ass again!" Kinston stormed out of the shop slamming the door behind him with such force that it bounced back open.

Barely able to move, all Charvette felt was pain surging through every inch of her body. Her left hand grappled for the phone cord, which was just within her reach. She yanked at the cord with the little strength she had, but it wasn't enough to displace the phone from the desktop before she completely passed out.

After being found and transported to the hospital, the damage to her neck and spine was quickly diagnosed. A team of doctors started surgery immediately to prevent permanent paralysis.

Favors

"Babe, I need you to do me a favor," Rossi started as soon as Micah answered her phone.

"Good morning to you too, Rossi," she answered.

"I'm sorry. How are you?" he asked quickly, trying to retract his rude and insensitive behavior.

"Yeah, yeah, yeah. What do you need?" she asked, her voice still heavy with sleep.

"I need you to call the florist and send some roses to my mom for her birthday. I forgot to do it yesterday. Hopefully, they can deliver them today."

Micah pulled herself up and leaned against her headboard, digesting Rossi's words. "Okay, hold on a minute. Let me get some paper and stuff." Fumbling over her clock radio, a glass of water that she'd been drinking the night before, and a book sitting on her night table, her fingers recognized the thin shape of a pen and a small pad of paper. "All right, where is it going?"

"Josephine Evans, ninety-three forty-three Yarborough Lane, Savannah, Georgia," he called out.

Micah jotted the address in an illegible hand-writing.

"What do you want to send?"

"Send umm . . . eighteen long-stemmed roses and see if they have some balloons that they can attach to it."

"What's your card number?" Micah asked as she ran her hand through her hair.

"Can you take care of it for me? I don't have my wallet with me. It's in the car. You know I don't like to bring it in the building."

Micah sighed loudly.

"Rossi, you know I just got back to work and I'm tryna catch up on my bills." *Selfish ass,* she kept to herself.

"I'll give it back to you," he promised. "I just don't have my wallet on me."

"You can't go out to your car and get it?"

"Not right now, babe. We're in the middle of a breakfast rush." When Micah didn't respond he spoke again, "Hello?"

"All this time you been on the phone with me you could have gone to your car."

"Baby, can you just please take care of it for me? I really don't have time to run out there."

"All right," Micah huffed, making sure that she tagged an audible and irritated sigh on the end.

"Thanks, babe," Rossi blurted, then gave her the name and number of the florist. "I'll give you a call a little bit later." At that, he hung up.

Micah did a cat stretch as she rose to her feet and padded to the bathroom for a shower think-ing about Rossi's call and how nice it was that he would send his mother flowers. Then she realized that only once had she ever received flowers of any type for any occasion from her fiancé. And those were only because he was trying to dig his way out of the doghouse.

Jealousy crept in and replaced the sleepiness that she washed away. Although she had no qualms about Rossi honoring his mother, and she loved the fact that he loved his mom so dearly, she had to ask herself why he hadn't ever done the same for her. As a matter of fact, what had he done for her last birthday? She traveled back in her mind, recalling spending the entire day at work running in circles waiting for some kind of a surprise that never came. Actually, the surprise was, he had given her nothing but a phone call.

"Hey, Granny," he had teased with laughter.

"Hey, Rossi," Micah had answered back a little less than excited. Her day had been coming to a close and it had been the first time she'd heard from Rossi all day. Her eyes had flitted upon an array of cards, helium-filled balloons, and varied gifts from her coworkers, along with a half-empty sheet-cake box that her supervisor had brought in to celebrate with her.

"Happy birthday," Rossi had said, still chuckling.

"Thanks."

"You busy?"

"Just trying to wrap up." Micah's response had been dry and unfeeling.

"Well, don't let me keep you. I just wanted to wish you a happy birthday."

"Thanks again," she had answered, then hung up. Two minutes of silence had passed as she had tried to reason why it had taken him all day to call. Coming up with no good answers, she had changed her focus, thinking that surely he had something amazing waiting for her once she got off work. To her disappointment, the phone call was the most she had received from him.

Micah's phone rang, bringing her back to the present. With her towel wrapped around her, she tiptoed back inside her bedroom and answered.

"I need to talk to you," Erin stated solemnly.

"Is everything okay?" Micah asked, detecting Erin's tone.

"Not really, but I'm okay. I just need a shoulder to cry on."

"Well, come on over. Just bring your gloves. Today is my gardening day."

"I'm on my way."

Micah pulled on a pair of old sweats and a T-shirt, inserted *"The Miseducation of Lauren Hill"* into her CD player, pressed the shuffle button, then began her cleaning routine by stripping the sheets from her bed and piling them in the washing machine. Lauren's words to "Ex-Factor" crept through the room and settled into Micah's mind as she sang along.

"See I know what we got to do, you let go and I'll let go too, 'cause no one's hurt me more than you. . . ."

As she tugged fresh sheets over her mattress, the notepad with the information she'd taken from Rossi earlier tumbled from her nightstand. With a sigh, she dialed the florist's number and gasped when she was quoted a price of $84.99 for the roses alone. Nonetheless, she placed the order and called out her credit card numbers, jotted down the confirmation number, and hung up the phone.

"He'd better give me my money back," she mumbled as she gathered a heap of clothes to take to the dry cleaners. After toting the garments downstairs, she placed them on her sofa then headed to the kitchen to start a pot of coffee, knowing Erin would arrive soon. Feeling inspired, she pulled out a bowl, a few eggs, and some frozen sausage patties to cook a small breakfast for the two of them to enjoy.

Before the sausages finished sizzling in the pan, Erin rang the doorbell.

"Come on in," Micah greeted. "I was just finishing up a little breakfast."

"I'm not hungry."

"Well, I cooked enough for the both of us, so you're going to have to find an appetite from somewhere."

Erin followed Micah to the kitchen and took a seat at the table. "It does smell kinda good in here," Erin acknowledged. "I guess I can nibble on a little something."

Micah put the food on two plates, set them on the table, poured two cups of coffee, then seated herself across from her friend. "So what's the sad face for?"

"Gideon and I broke up," she released, using that as the intro for the news she was leading up to. She pressed the side of her fork into her sausage patty.

"What do you mean you broke up? You two have been together for, like, two years," Micah exclaimed in disbelief.

"I mean, we broke up. I dismissed him from my life."

"Because?"

"He was cheating on me." There was a dormant pause as Micah gave an expression that could easily be read as "I told you that already." Erin nodded with an affirmative expression. "But that's not the worst of it." It was then that her eyes began to water. "He also gave me an STD. . . ." she trailed, indicating in her tone that there was more. "HPV," she finished.

Micah put her fork down and bit her lip as she remembered the "One Less" commercials she'd seen on television promoting HPV prevention, and the awareness ads she'd seen. "Erin, I'm sorry."

"So am I. For trusting someone else with my own health." She rearranged the eggs on her plate with her fork. "I've been to the doctor two times for Pap smear testing since my routine one came back abnormal. The other tests came back showing that I have type sixteen."

"What does that mean?"

"It means I could develop cervical cancer."

"What?!" Micah was completely shocked, as she'd never paid much attention to the HPV information that she'd been exposed to. "Cancer?" Erin nodded slowly. "What's the treatment for it?"

"There's a vaccination that I can get, but it's not guaranteed, especially since I've already contracted it and there's no cure for it."

"There's got to be something you can do, Erin. Can't they freeze off the cancerous cells or something like that?"

"I don't know," she replied in her most defeated tone.

"Uhn-uh, Erin, I am not about to let you sit here and go into a depression when we can take action and find out everything there is to know about what we can do," Micah said, jumping to her feet. "Are you finished eating? We have somewhere to go," she announced, grasping the edge of Erin's plate.

"I don't feel like going anywhere."

"I know you don't, but you're going anyway," she ordered. She placed both their unfinished breakfast plates on the counter. "When did you find this out?"

"The day before yesterday."

"Okay, and that is more than enough time for you to have sat around trying to grasp the news. Now, we're going to beat it down like it stole something. Get your purse," Micah directed as she opened her front closet and pulled out a pair of tennis shoes.

"Where are we going?"

"Have you ever heard the saying 'If you want to keep something from a black man, put it in a book'? Well, we're about to make a liar out of somebody. Let's go." Without another thought, she grabbed her purse, keys, laptop, and Erin's wrist and headed for the library. "You can beat this, Erin. I know you can. And I'm going to help you."

While Micah drove downtown, she thought about the money she'd spent on the roses for Rossi's mom and compared it to what Erin had just shared with her. Her disappointments with Rossi all seemed so petty now. Birthday gifts, or the lack thereof, seemed so trivial. Getting a phone call or getting stood up was far better than getting an STD that could result in cancer.

Later that day, Micah pulled out her cell phone and dialed Rossi at work. Once he answered, she opened her heart. "Hey, Rossi."

"Hey," he rushed.

"I just called to tell you I love you," she sincerely whispered.

There was an unexpected silence before Rossi responded. "Did you send those flowers to my mother?" Speechless and feeling foolish, Micah pressed her lips together and hung up the phone.

Just Looking

Stephen pulled up in front of Micah's home, checked his mirror once more, then stepped out of his vehicle.

"This is not a date. This is not a date," he reminded himself. "Show her the properties and move on." Even though he coached himself, he still felt a flutter of excitement knowing that he and Micah would spend the afternoon together. He had carefully drawn out an itinerary that would ensure that the last property they viewed would be at least forty-five minutes away from her home. By the time they would finish there, he hoped she'd be hungry enough to agree to grab a bite to eat.

With a touch of nervousness, he rang the bell and was greeted seconds later by Micah's stunning appearance. She smiled politely as she unlocked her storm door, then pushed it open to let him in the entrance hallway.

"Hey, Stephen, come on in. I'll just be a minute."

"Sure, no problem." Stephen struggled to keep

a smile from forming on his face and quickly grabbed and glanced at his cell phone to distract himself from watching her sprint up the stairs. He scrolled through a list of previously read text messages to kill the next minute or so until Micah returned.

"Sorry about that. I just needed to wrap up something. I'm ready," she said, pulling her purse up on her shoulder.

Stephen measured his next words carefully, not wanting to seem too forward. "Did you want to ride along with me, or follow me in your car?" He paused for only a split second. "I have air-conditioning and a James Brown greatest hits CD," he joked as a teaser.

"Well, since you put it that way, who could ever turn down the opportunity to be entertained by James mumbling over horns?" She laughed. "I guess I could ride along with you," she agreed.

Yes! "Cool. Let me get the door for you," Stephen replied, seemingly unfazed by her response.

Once she was seated on the passenger's side, he took his seat and smoothly pulled away. As he'd promised, James was crooning about having soul and being super bad, but he turned the music down slightly to brief her on the properties.

"Okay, so what I have here are all single-family homes, all in excess of three thousand square feet, at least five bedrooms, which should accommodate your present needs and your future plans for a family." He paused pensively as if to recall other property features. *Why is it the good women are always taken, he questioned himself.* "Most have two-car garages, which you mentioned was important to you, and you mentioned your fiancé being interested in lot size, so a few of them have quite a bit of land, while the others aren't so generous. I'm sorry he couldn't join us to take a look," he said. Truthfully, he was grateful that, as Micah had slightly complained about, Rossi was too busy to fit the home viewings in his schedule.

"He trusts my judgment, and of course we will revisit any that I really like." Micah was actually seething that once again Rossi had put her on the back burner, but she covered it with a gleaming smile. "I'll be taking notes."

"Most couples are able to gauge what their significant other will like, so I'm sure you'll make some good decisions about the homes that I'll show you."

They toured the six homes Stephen had selected, and he pointed out each home's amenities. As Micah expressed her likes and dislikes, through her comments and facial gestures, Stephen was careful to jot them down in her file, to make better future selections, in the event that none of the properties really suited her liking.

Micah seemed to be particularly taken with one home that featured a luxurious Jacuzzi sunken in a marble floor. "Oh my goodness!" she gasped as she stepped down into the tub, comfortably sized for two. "This is incredible," she added following her urge to take a seat, lean back against the spotless fiberglass, and close her eyes. She let out a slow moan as if she could actually feel the circulation of hot water enveloping her and Rossi.

"I don't know if I should be standing here while you are nestling in the tub so comfortably." Stephen chuckled, wishing that he could join her, although they were both fully clothed. "So I'm going to wait for you out here in the bedro . . . uh, in the kitchen."

"Okay. I promise I won't be long," she answered, not bothering to open her eyes.

With rapid steps Stephen exited the oversized lavatory to hide his arousal. "Mmph, mmph, mmph," he commented to himself once out of her hearing range. "My man'd better watch his back," he said, struggling against his moral values, knowing that per her own subtle remarks, Rossi wasn't on his A game. "That man is a stone-cold fool," he chuckled, pondering whether there was a chance Micah could be whisked away. He patiently leaned against the countertop and folded his arms across his chest as he was reminded of the familiar saying "Where there's a will, there's a way."

Back in the bathroom, Micah envisioned a multitude of bubbles covering everything but her and Rossi's faces, even hiding her long tresses and his bald head. In her one-minute fantasy, Rossi sat opposite her massaging her feet and gingerly sucking her toes. A plate of fresh strawberries sat on the floor at the tub's entrance, which Rossi dipped into a fondue pot of white chocolate, then reached across and fed her. After sharing bites of the strawberries, Rossi coaxed her over to him and made love to her.

"You all right in there?" Stephen called from the other room, bringing her daydream to a close as she popped her eyes open.

"Yeah, I'm fine," she responded, lifting herself from the hollow, then stepping up onto the floor. "That would be so nice," she whispered to herself, turned on by her thoughts. Right away she began making plans to seduce Rossi that night, despite her own convictions to never sleep with him again. "I think I've found the house," Micah commented as she joined Stephen in the kitchen after touring the remainder of the house alone.

"The bathtub was quite impressive," he commented. "If I were in the market for a home, I think I would seriously contemplate making an offer on this one myself."

"Speaking of, how long has it been on the market?"

"About a month or so," he responded as he thumbed through a few sheets of paper he held in his hand. "It looks like the sellers couldn't get their original asking price for it and had to make a few changes. The price dropped by a couple grand earlier this week, but even so, it's not been getting that much activity," he added, pointing out the couple of realtors' business cards that had been left on the kitchen counter. "It's a nice piece of property."

"Yes, it is." Micah nodded, glancing out the kitchen window into the backyard. "This one is definitely on my comeback list."

"So you think your fiancé will like it, then," Stephen said more as a statement than a question.

"I'm going to do all I can to make him like it," Micah said with a flicker of seduction that was enough to cause Stephen's loins to leap. He cleared his throat nervously before speaking again.

"Well, there are two more on the list that I wanted you to take a look at, unless you know this is the one."

"Oh, this is the one," she said confidently. "We can stop right now. As a matter of fact, I'm about to starve. Do you mind stopping somewhere where I can get a cheeseburger, a chicken sandwich, a slice of bread—something!" she exclaimed, running a hand across her belly.

"Not a problem at all." Stephen smiled. "I'm kinda hungry myself." He added his business card to the others, then led the way to the front door. "Please let me get your door for you."

"Oh, that won't be necessary. I can get it."

"Micah, I insist. It's the gentlemanly thing to do," he said, stopping for a moment to turn toward her. "Please let me be a gentleman." Micah pressed her lips together in a half smile and kept silent, only signaling with her brows that she'd submit to his request. He let her out and secured the property, then seconds later, escorted her to his car. "So what do you have a taste for?" he said, opening her door.

"I'm not choosy." She shrugged. "Hungry but not choosy." She looked over at Stephen and caught his half smile as their eyes met. In an instant she looked away to conceal an oncoming blush, although no words were spoken.

"How much time do you have?" he chanced.

Micah shrugged a second time. "I'm in no rush. Why, what do you have in mind?"

"Nothing really," he answered, although that was far from the truth, but he was careful not to be too forward. After all, she was engaged to be married, so she said. "Just wanted to get a feel for if you wanted to grab some fast food or sit down somewhere. Either one is fine with me, but I understand that you might need to get home to your fiancé." In his peripheral vision, he noted Micah's immediate change in expression as she rolled her eyes and turned her head to look out the window.

"I'm in no rush. As a matter of fact, I could use a sit-down meal while we discuss all of my options," she responded.

"Well, give me a minute to think," he said, internalizing his grin. "Do you eat Chinese?" he asked, reasoning that the food would be filling and the setting wouldn't be overly intimate.

"Yes, I do, regardless of the cat, dog, and rat rumors." She giggled.

"There's nothing wrong with a little cat-fried rice," he joked. "I've been eating it pretty much all my life and I'm fine."

Yes, you are, Micah kept to herself.

"There's a place down on Broad Street that we can run in," he suggested.

"Sounds good to me."

Micah's plate was piled with chow mein noodles, orange chicken, beef and broccoli, and steamed vegetables. A smaller plate held slices of watermelon and orange, sided with a few plump strawberries. Stephen met her at the table with a full plate of his own.

"You really were hungry, huh?" he commented, looking down at her food.

"I see you're quite famished yourself," she egged in return.

"See, I like you already. You're not ashamed to get your eat on when you know you starving." He stabbed a spicy piece of General Tso's Chicken, then gathered some rice and forked it into his mouth. After a few solid chews he continued, "Most women try to do that salad thing Eddie Murphy talked about back in the day."

"What salad thing?" Micah inquired.

"You don't remember 'Raw'?" he asked in an attempt to jog her memory.

"Raw? Was that some movie he did or something?"

"You can't be serious!" he said, then began to chuckle. "Micah, how old are you, if you don't mind me asking?"

"Twenty-six, and don't even act like you are so much older than me."

"I have at least cleared my twenties. Although there is nothing wrong with being in your twenties. I can't believe you don't know anything about Eddie back in the day."

Micah twisted her lips to one side as she raised her eyebrows and commented, "Nope."

"Well, before the days of *Shrek I, II,* and *III* and *Dreamgirls,* my man Eddie did this stand-up routine called "Raw." You're gonna have to watch it— it's hilarious."

"I did see *Dreamgirls,*" Micah perked before bursting out in song. "Jimmy got soul, Jimmy got soul, Jimmy got, Jimmy got, Jimmy got soul!" They both broke into a fit of laughter, each one catching the sparkle the other's eyes held.

"Leave Jimmy alone. He was trying to get his ratings up after Jamie Foxx shot his song down." With a rich, mellow voice, Stephen began singing out lyrics to "Patience" as he used his fork to beat out a rhythm on the table.

"You are crazy!" Micah laughed but joined in with him seconds later.

They stopped themselves once they couldn't remember any more words or memorable scenes. Stephen rose to his feet. "Want some ice cream? You know it soothes the stomach after a meal like this."

"Mmmm . . ." Micah contemplated.

"Come on, you know you want to."

"I do, but I have a dress to fit into in a few months," she responded, causing a rift in Stephen's previously jovial mood.

He hid the slight twinge of envy he felt at the mention of her pending marriage as he blurted, "I'm sure you're going to be gorgeous . . . even with a little ice cream. Nobody will even notice. Just have a little." Then he added, "I'll pay for your food. . . ." dragging his last word teasingly.

Micah burst into laughter again. "That's all you had to say!" She stood and followed Stephen to the soft-serve machine, swirled the smooth treat into a small bowl, then garnished it with a sprinkle of crushed M&Ms. Stephen topped his ice cream with a spoonful of pineapple, and then they both made their way to their table, which had been cleaned off by the time they returned.

"So you're pretty excited about your wedding, huh?" Stephen fished.

Micah found it hard to lie. "Umm . . . actually, planning a wedding is kind of stressful," she said in place of sharing how unsure she was of marrying Rossi. "There're lots of decisions to be made, lots of things to think about that I never even imagined. And it's expensive as all get-out," she ended. "What about you? There's no special somebody somewhere looking forward to the day that she becomes your wife?"

"No. If there is, I don't know anything about it," he dismissed as he spooned the combination of yellow and white into his mouth.

"Do you think you would ever want to get married?"

"Sure. I think everybody wants somebody to love and to love them back. Just like my boy Teddy said." Stephen started to sing a second time: "It's so good loving somebody—" He stopped abruptly. "Oh, wait, that's probably before your time," he joked.

"And somebody loves you back!" Micah finished, with a smile. "See there smarty-pants. I do
know a little something."

"I'm impressed." He smiled at her. Silence hung
in the air for two seconds before he cleared his
throat and spoke again. "But yeah, I would like to
get married. I would want to fly somewhere to a
beautiful white sandy beach and blue sky and the
beauty of God's handiwork as the decorative backdrop for my wedding," he shared.

"Really?"

"Yeah. It's just something I love about being outdoors. When my sister got married a few years
back, she spent so much money on flowers it was
ridiculous. Brought them all indoors, scattered
them all over the church and reception hall, and
they all died the next day. She could have let those
flowers stay outside, had all the scenery she
wanted, and kept it moving."

"So you want to be outside for the sake of the
life span of a few roses?" Micah asked.

"No, it's not that. I just love the great outdoors,
and those tropical locations are really beautiful.
People are always having church weddings to be
closer to God and all that, but how much closer
can you be than to have the sky as the ceiling, the
earth as the floor, and His plants and flowers as
the decorations?"

"You know, I never thought about it like that."
Micah rested her chin in her palm as she leaned an
elbow on the table. "You make a good point there."

"Well maybe one day I'll get to live that out, but
right now I guess I'd better get you back home
before your man comes looking for me," he said,
pushing his empty bowl away. "You ready?"

"Yeah." Micah reached for her purse and dug for her wallet.

"Don't worry about that; I've got it," he said, insistent that she not spend any money.

"Let me at least leave the tip," she pressed.

"No can do," Stephen responded, pulling a ten-dollar bill from his pocket and tossing it on the table. "I can't let you spend a single dime. It was my pleasure to dine with you this evening. Paying for it is the least I can do."

Again Micah found herself grinning in approval of his behavior. "You think you can call my fiancé and give him lessons?"

"If he needs lessons, he doesn't deserve you," he commented, giving Micah something to think about.

The two rode back to Micah's home in silence with Stephen wishing he could have Micah, and Micah reevaluating her relationship. As his car came to a stop in front of her house, he quickly let himself out, jetted to the opposite side of the car, and opened her door for her.

"I'll wait to hear from you about the properties we looked at," he said, nodding.

"Okay. I'll give you a call sometime tomorrow, I guess." She dug in her purse to locate her keys, purposely avoiding eye contact.

"Thanks for a great evening, by the way. It was fun."

Their eyes locked as Micah responded, "Yeah, it was."

Stephen resisted the urge to lean into Micah, though he longed to plant a soft kiss on her lips, imagining what it would be like to hold her in his arms. Instead, he watched her walk to her front door, then threw up a single hand as she waved from the door. He backed out of her driveway trying to think of what he could do to whisk her away from another man's arms.

Once inside her house, Micah sighed, reflecting on the past few hours. Stephen had been the perfect gentleman as well as good company over dinner. *Now why can't Rossi act like that?* Although she enjoyed being with Stephen, she did feel guilty about wasting his time looking at homes when she had no intention of staying in the area.

Help Wanted

Micah dragged her suitcase to the rental car counter, blurted her reservation number, and minutes later headed to the lot with a set of keys to a Pontiac Grand Am. The flight to Charlotte had taken less than an hour, but already Micah felt relief from her usual day's worth of pressure. To give herself an opportunity to scope the Charlotte area, Micah had opted to take a temporary assignment of assisting the Charlotte site during its ramp-up phase. She'd spend the next four weeks interviewing management staff candidates, then facilitating training. Not only did it give her an opportunity to escape the mundane details of her work life, but it provided the break from Rossi that she felt she needed. She was hoping that her temporary absence would cause both their hearts to grow a little fonder.

She reflected back on earlier that morning when he'd dropped her off at the airport. They'd rode in complete silence, he hadn't bothered to help her pull her luggage out of the back of her truck, and no sooner than she lowered the last suitcase to the ground he sped off without so much as a simple good-bye. Had it not been for his long list of growing relationship infractions, Micah would have been offended. But instead, it only made her more inspired about the true motivating factor of her trip.

It was only ten o'clock on Saturday morning, and not having to report to work until Monday afternoon, Micah planned to spend the next two days simply relaxing and having some quality self-preservation time. She'd already planned to spend her Sunday at Carmel Day Spa, for a full-package pampering to include a European facial, a manicure with a moisturizing hand treatment, a pedicure, an exfoliating body wrap, a one-hour Swedish massage, and lunch. The package also included a haircut, but there was no way Micah would trust unknown hands with her crown of glory.

Afterward, she'd spend some time at poolside catching up on some reading. Blair Underwood's *Casanegra,* nestled alongside Lori Bryant-Woolridge's *Weapons of Mass Seduction,* poked out from the top of her shoulder bag. She doubted she'd be able to read them both while she was there, but she'd at least get started on one of them. As for today, she planned to do a little shopping, which always seemed to be the perfect cure whenever she felt less than her best emotionally.

After finding her way to I-77, she cruised to exit 25 to visit Birkdale Village. The urban village setting of shops, luxury apartments, offices, restaurants, and a movie theater made the perfect backdrop for her desire for a leisurely Saturday afternoon. Sitting down to an afternoon meal of a grilled chicken salad covered with a spicy honey mustard dressing, she finally switched her cell phone back on from having it off during her flight. Within seconds her voice mail indicator chimed, prompting her to check her messages.

"Micah, it's Stephen. I hope you had a safe flight today. I just wanted to let you know that I found a couple more properties that I thought you and your fiancé would be interested in. I know you'll be out of town for a while, but please give me a call at your earliest convenience. Maybe your fiancé can take a look at the houses. I look forward to hearing from you."

"Hey, it's Rossi. Call me when you land. Don't get down there and forget that you're engaged."

What is that supposed to mean? she thought, rolling her eyes and deleting the message. "No ring, no engagement," she uttered under her breath. With a bit of attitude, she dialed Rossi's number, hoping for his voice mail rather than his live voice. She was relieved when his voice mail picked up after four rings.

"Hey, babe, just wanted to let you know that I made it safely. The real estate guy might call you to look at a couple of houses. Let me know what you think of them. I'll call you in a little while."

She dialed Stephen's number next. "Hi, Stephen. I got your message, and yeah, while I am out of town, you can give Rossi a call and have him view the properties you've found. I will be here in Charlotte for about four weeks, so you'll definitely have to get with him. You can also e-mail me with any listings or photos." She finished her message sharing both her and Rossi's information.

* * *

Monday afternoon came far too quickly, but Micah was well rested and ready to do her job. After meeting the managing director, Gerald Stone, and the senior director, Kaycee Frederick, Micah went straight to work at not just interviewing and training, but more so of making a good impression and building a solid networking relationship with both Gerald and Kaycee.

By week's end, Micah and Kaycee had become acquainted enough to plan a shopping excursion that Saturday. Kaycee swung by the hotel in her Chrysler 300 to pick Micah up, and the two ladies headed out for a little "plastic" therapy.

"So have you thought about maybe relocating to this area, Micah? We could use your strength and talent on our team," Kaycee started, maneuvering her head to swing a face full of black curls out of her way. "I don't know why I just didn't put this stuff in a ponytail." Kaycee dug through her Guess Kokomo Bucket purse. Locating a black scrunchie with her fingers, she pulled it out of the bag and secured her hair at the nape of her neck.

"I thought about it a little bit, but I'm supposed to be getting married soon and it would definitely have to be a decision that we'd make together," Micah shared.

"Oh," Kaycee said with surprise. "I didn't realize you were engaged." She took a naturally reflexive glance at Micah's left hand, inadvertently causing a wave of embarrassment to wash over Micah. "Do you have kids?"

"No, not yet. I think I'd like to have a couple, but you know the saying . . . first comes love . . . and I don't think I've got that part figured out yet," Micah freely confessed.

"What do you mean? You aren't sure if you love him?"

"No, I'm not sure if he loves *me*."

"I'm sure he does if he asked you to marry him."

"You would think that would be the case, but"—Micah shook her head in doubt—"sometimes I just don't know."

"Well, has he told you he loves you?"

"Yeah, he says it occasionally, but to be honest with you, I can't really say that his actions are convincing."

"Do you think he's cheating or something?" Kaycee asked, prying.

"Well, I wouldn't go so far as to say that, but sometimes I just don't know. I mean, my finger is still empty, for starters," Micah complained.

"Maybe he's still looking for the perfect ring," she suggested.

"That could be it, but I don't think so. I just feel strung along."

"Well, take it from me, girl, if it don't feel good now, it's not going to feel good later. It will only get worse. If you're having doubts, do yourself a favor and don't do it."

"So you're married I take it?"

"Girl, divorced twice. And the thing about it is, I loved being married. I think I'd even do it one more time," Kaycee stated as she wheeled into the parking lot of South Park Mall.

"So what happened?"

"Just didn't work out." She shrugged. "One had 'baby momma' drama; he thought I was going to sit back and let that wench run my house. And you know I won't havin' that." She parked the car and gathered her purse. "After we leave here, we need to go to Blacklion. Girl, they have awesome stuff in there. Anyway, the second one took a liking to preteens." Micah gasped in disbelief. "Yeah, girl. That messed me all up. Girl, just broke my confidence in men altogether."

"That's terrible," Micah commented, recalling some of her own experiences and scars from being raised in the foster care system. "Well, I'm definitely ready to get my shop on," she said, changing the subject quickly. "I don't even want to think about men right now. I'll deal with that can of worms when I get home."

"Rossi, you need to come home as soon as possible," Romni said in sobs. She'd journeyed back to Georgia after calling Josephine two weeks before and finding out that her health was failing. "It's Momma. Her sugar dropped and she had to be rushed to the hospital from her job."

"What are they saying? Is she okay?" Rossi said in panic.

"I don't know. They didn't give me her condition, but just said that someone needed to get there right away 'cause she might go into a coma, so I'm on my way there now."

"I'll be there as soon as I can." He flipped his phone closed, turned to his computer, and immediately booked a flight to Savannah, Georgia, as a flurry of thoughts spun in his head. He wondered if his mother had been keeping up on her insulin shots, as she had many times been instructed to do so, but often failed. He called out for one of his assistant managers as he packed his desk up for the day.

"Susan, I'm going to have to leave early today and will be out for the next couple of days for a family emergency."

"Is everything okay?"

"I'm not sure just yet. My mom was just admitted to the hospital."

Susan gasped before she continued. "I'm sorry to hear that. What do you need from me?" She jotted down a list of directives and agreed to make sure everything was taken care of as Rossi rushed out the door and headed to the parking lot.

Glancing at his watch, he pressed his foot on the gas pedal even more, because he had to go home and pack clothes. An hour later he was headed to the airport. As he drove, he dialed Micah's number.

"Hey, babe," he started in his normal fashion.

"Hi, Rossi."

"Listen, I'm having to catch the next flight out to Georgia this afternoon. My mom's been rushed to the hospital."

"Oh no! Is she all right? What happened?"

"I don't have all of the details just yet, but she had a drop in her blood sugar, and they are thinking she might go into a coma—if she hasn't already—so I'm headed down there."

"I hope everything is okay, Rossi," Micah spoke sympathetically. "I know I'm out of town, but if there is anything I can do, just let me know."

"Right now I don't know if there is anything anybody can do other than the doctors and God," he replied, becoming choked on his words. He cleared his throat in an effort to maintain his composure.

"I can at the very least pray," she said sincerely.

"Thank you, Micah. I appreciate that."

"You're welcome."

"I'll call you once I get there and see what's going on."

"Okay. Be safe, Rossi."

"I will," he answered, then added, "I love you, Micah."

"I love you too, Rossi." She bit her lower lip, feeling a twinge of guilt. After the poor response he gave her the last time she'd uttered those words, she'd vowed to herself that they'd never cross her lips again. But at the moment, she believed that it was absolutely the right thing to say.

Several hours later, drained of all physical and emotional strength, Rossi sat at Josephine's dining room table. His heart had been broken the evening before when he'd witnessed his mother lying in a comatose state, hooked to various machines, unable to do anything more than breathe. He had stood and sat at her bedside for close to ninety minutes simply washing her face and hands with his tears. "Momma, please don't make me do this. Please wake up," he'd mumbled in a sob. "Please."

He'd spent the night slumped in a chair in the waiting room, covered by a thin blanket, praying for positive change and dreaming of days gone by. When morning had come, he had driven his rented Toyota Corolla to his mother's house and landed in an exhausted, crumpled heap onto the sofa.

Now here he sat in a total daze, his thoughts blurred, as he reread the words printed on his mother's living will. He'd been studying the one-page document for over two hours now, not knowing how he would get through carrying out Josephine's wishes. Although he could recite the words, they still had not quite sunk in:

1. *I direct my attending physician to withhold or withdraw life-sustaining treatment that serves only to prolong the process of my dying if I should be in an incurable or irreversible mental or physical condition with no clear and solid expectation of recovery beyond five days.*
2. *In the event of a coma, the same directive should apply.*
3. *I direct that treatment be limited to measures to keep me comfortable and to relieve pain, including any pain that might occur by withholding or withdrawing life- sustaining treatment.*
4. *I designate Rossi Evans of Richmond, Virginia, as my surrogate to make medical treatment decisions for me in a manner consistent with this declaration if I should be incompetent and in a terminal condition or in a state of permanent unconsciousness. If the person I have named above is unable to act on my behalf, I authorize the following person to do so: Romni Evans of Savannah, Georgia.*

Rossi ran a single hand across his face and rubbed hard. It was the second day that Josephine had been in a comatose state and the minutes were passing far too quickly. He revisited in his mind Dr. Fosmio's words from the day before. *"It's just one of those things that we can't predict. I've seen people come through in a few days, and others who lie in bed for years."* He forced himself to his feet, walked to the refrigerator, pulled out a bottle of orange juice, and took a long swig straight from the bottle. Attached to the refrigerator door was the same Mother's Day card that had hung there for more than twenty years now. It was a simple folded sheet of what was once white paper, but had yellowed with time, with Rossi's tiny handprint traced in red crayon. *I Love You Mom!* was scribbled in his kindergarten penmanship. A wave of emotions began to overcome him. First grief; just the thought of burying his mother was more than he could bear. Then anger that she had put him in the horrible position of giving the doctors the go-ahead to end her life. Regret was next, as he thought about his last conversation with his mom.

"When you coming home to see your momma?"

"Ma, don't start that mess today. You know I'm busy," he'd huffed.

"You still got a momma who you can come see about every now and then." Her voice had become more shaky as she'd spoken. "I know you busy, but you don't have to be so mean."

"And you don't have to be so needy, Ma."

"Well, excuuuuuse me!" Josephine had said through tears. "I just wanted to see your face one more time before I died. But you know what? Don't you worry about me, hear? I'll be all right."

"Ma, I'm not saying . . ."

"No, I heard what you said, Rossi. I'm sorry for bothering you today. Call me when you got some time for your momma." Josephine had hung up before Rossi could utter another word.

That day had been more than six months ago. And though Rossi, consumed with guilt, had sent his mother money, cards, and gifts, he had never lifted the phone to call and apologize. Now he would never get that opportunity.

Regardless, he whispered aloud, "I'm sorry, Momma. Please forgive me." His words merged into silent sobbing as he took a seat in the middle of the kitchen floor and tucked his head between his knees. Ten minutes later, still seated on the floor, he tightened the laces of his tennis shoes, then darted out the back door. As soon as his feet hit the pavement, he took off running and didn't stop until he'd reached the doors of the hospital—thirteen miles from Josephine's front doorstep.

Not caring that he was drenched with sweat, he entered through the hospital's front doors then looked around for a sign pointing to a bathroom. He pushed open the door, walked to the sink, and splashed water on his face, then studied his reflection in the mirror. His T-shirt was darkened with perspiration and his face looked worn and worried. His dark eyes revealed the guilt that consumed him, feeling as if he could have done something—anything—that could have prevented both his mother and himself from being in such a horrible predicament.

"What to do, what to do," he whispered as he stared down the drain of the porcelain bowl in front of him. "I don't know what to do, God," he prayed, dropping tears into the sink as he folded his lips into his mouth. He continued to pray out loud: "Lord, you said you'd never put more on me than I could bear . . . and this is too heavy for me. How can I make this decision?" Rossi took a long, contemplative pause. "I can't. I can't do it. And it's not right for her to ask me to," he concluded. Then a passage of Scripture that he remembered from Sunday school popped in his head. *Children, obey your parents in the Lord: for this is right. Honour*

*thy father and mother; which is the first commandment
with promise; that it may be well with thee, and thou
mayest live long on the earth.* "Ephesians six one
through three," he spoke. "You're gonna have to
help me with this one." After patting his face with
a wet paper towel, he inhaled deeply and blew out
the air through puckered lips. Taking a final look
at himself before leaving, he told God once more,
"Yeah. I'ma need your help with this one here."

Rossi splashed water on his face once more, then
exited the bathroom to go upstairs. It seemed to take
him both too long and too quick to arrive on the
second floor where ICU was located. Stopping at the
nurses' station, he asked for the doctor on duty.

"Whom are you here to see, sir?" the woman
asked.

"Josephine Evans," he replied, with flutters in
his stomach.

"Just a minute," the woman stated and flipped
through a few patient charts filed against the wall.
"Only immediate family members are allowed to
see Ms. Evans right now. Are you an immediate
family member?"

"I'm her son," Rossi stated, reaching for his
wallet to make his ID available.

With a quick glance at Rossi's driver's license,
she recognized him as the decision maker. "The
doctor is not available right now, but you can go in
and see your mom."

"How is she doing?" he asked somberly.

"She's actually making progress," she commented as she reviewed the chart. "She came out of
her coma about two hours ago, but she still has a
ways to go."

"Really?" Rossi's eyes stretched as he felt his
stomach tumble, and then he blew out a long sigh.

"You can go in for a little while, but she needs plenty of rest." The nurse placed the chart back in the hanging file, then pointed toward the room with her hand. "She's still there in two-oh-seven."

"Thank you," Rossi whispered in relief. With shaky fingers he put his license back in his wallet and took measured steps toward the suite where Josephine lay.

Rossi didn't attempt to hide his tears as he looked down upon his mother sleeping fitfully in her hospital bed. He stroked a hand across her hair, then let his finger trail down her face. He studied the deep wrinkles that seemed to have suddenly settled around her eyes and mouth. Since the last time he'd seen her, her youthfulness had slipped away. Today she looked twenty years older than she had at the family reunion. *How has she aged so quickly?* he thought. Josephine stirred slightly at his touch before her eyes fluttered open and then focused on her son.

"Thank you for the roses," she whispered, with a strained smile. Quickly Rossi wiped his tears away. "How long you been here, baby?" she whispered.

"Not long." Rossi lightly grabbed his mother's hand. "How are you feeling today?"

"I don't know." She shook her head slowly and closed her eyes for a few seconds. "It's kinda hard to figure out when you're lying flat on your back and can barely move." She paused as she closed her eyes in thought. "Right now my whole head is full of coulda-woulda-shouldas. It's a terrible thing to look back over your life and all you can see is a sea of regrets." Tears began to seep from the corners of her eyes and roll back onto her pillow. "I tell you what, though. If I ever get out this bed," she promised, stretching the word *ever* for a full two seconds, "I'm gone live."

"Shhh," Rossi coaxed. "Please don't get yourself all roused up." He kissed the back of her hand, then ran a hand over her disheveled curly hair.

"You still a young man, baby," she continued, despite her son's plea for her to rest. "You better live while you got the chance . . . and make it worth something. Have you something to look back on and smile about, hear?"

"Yes ma'am," he responded respectfully.

Rossi stayed another thirty minutes until Josephine drifted off to sleep again, wishing there was something he could do to see his mother well, but left her room incredibly grateful that she had pulled through and that he would not have to make a decision that surely would have affected him for the rest of his life. Startled by the vibration of his cell phone, he reached into his pants pocket and answered, seeing that it was Micah.

"Everything okay, baby?" Micah asked.

"Uh . . ." Rossi choked on his words momentarily. "Mom is much better, but still is not out of the woods yet. I'm just glad that she's still here."

Micah thought carefully on what she could say to Rossi, knowing that mere words could hardly change things. "Things are going to be all right."

"Yeah." Seconds of silence passed. "I'll call you back in a little bit. I have some thinking to do," he said somberly. He took the stairs to the ground floor still thinking about Josephine's words. Was he leaving a trail of regrets behind him? The more he thought, the more he recognized gaps in his life that required his attention, the main one being Micah. There was no doubt in his mind that he loved her, and she loved him. And now, it didn't make sense to him why he had convinced her to postpone their wedding. Suddenly inspired, he called a cab and made plans to go back to his childhood home, take a shower, and head for the jewelry store. He'd put Micah off for long enough.

A few hours and a few thousand dollars later, he smiled to himself, ready to fully claim the woman he'd call his wife.

Josephine's progression was rapid and she was able to be released from the hospital within the next week. Rossi assisted her into his vehicle and cautiously drove her home in silence, not finding any words to speak other than telling her he loved her, which he'd done numerous times that morning already.

"It sure is good to be among the land of the living," she said, looking out the window.

"And it's good to have you still here, Momma." Rossi reached over and patted Josephine's knee.

"I got one more day to tell God thank you. You just don't know when your last time will be."

Rossi nodded silently. "Momma, you remember the girl I brought down to the family reunion?"

"Who, Micah?" she recalled, surprising Rossi.

"You remembered her name?"

"Micah was a prophet in the Bible, you know. I don't forget stuff like that."

"Well, I'm going to ask her to marry me," he announced.

"Oh yeah?"

"Yes, ma'am." He nodded. "I'll have to show you the ring I got her," he said, keeping his eyes on the road. "I'm going to propose when I get home," he added, glancing over at his mother. He chuckled to himself as he realized she had in a matter of seconds drifted off to sleep.

Return to Sender!

Rossi nearly collapsed on his couch after removing his shoes just inside his front door. Totally exhausted from working extra overtime hours all week since his return from Georgia, all he wanted to do was shower and sleep, but he thought he'd rest a minute before pressing toward the bathroom.

With the mail in one hand, he reached forward to grab the remote from the coffee table and turned on the television. He half watched an episode of MTV's *Making the Band* featuring Diddy while he thumbed through the stack of envelopes.

Rossi skipped past the utility bills and let his fingers rest on an envelope that seemed to be a letter. There was no return address, but the postmark indicated that it had been mailed from a neighboring city. He slid his finger through the seal and pulled out a single folded sheet of paper with handwriting on it.

Rossi,
I know you told me that things were over, but I felt there needed to be some closure in our lives . . . at

least in mine. I thought what we shared was special and something that would be cherished by the both of us. I understand now that we can never be together, and I am willing to accept that and move on with my life.

When you came over a few weeks back to talk to me about your problems with Micah, I thought that maybe we could pick up where we'd left off. I guess in my determination to have you to myself, I did everything I could to make her life miserable, hoping that she'd in turn make you miserable enough to run to me. It was painful to sit at her desk, where she has pictures of the both of you everywhere. Pictures of you smiling with her, holding her . . . kissing her. I only said what I said to her at the club out of my jealousy that she had you and I didn't. You don't know how it broke my heart when my phone calls to you went unanswered and unreturned. I was a fool thinking what barely even got off the ground would last forever. I didn't realize until the other night when you were here how much I still love you. I already know what you are going to say—that what happened between us was a mistake that never should have taken place. And although you couldn't stay long, that night is still fresh in my memory. Maybe you have erased it from your mind, but what I felt and experienced when we made love will never leave my soul. As a matter of fact, I've never forgotten about you and I just wanted you to know.

Good luck with your life, and I hope things work out between you and Micah if that is whom you ultimately decide to be with. Know that you will always be in my heart.

I love you, Rossi.

Jaison Anthony McDonald

Rossi, though tired, jumped to his feet to head toward the kitchen to immediately burn the letter over the sink. "You ain't gone get me caught out there," he mumbled.

"What's up, Jai Mac?" Rossi greeted, slapping hands with Jaison Anthony McDonald as the two passed each other in the stairwell of one of the nine buildings of Copeley Apartments, which offered double-occupancy living quarters for upperclassmen.

"Whassup, Ros?" Anthony replied, dragging a large duffel bag of dirty clothes behind him.

"This business and political economy is kicking my butt, man," Rossi huffed as he hoisted his backpack up on his shoulder. His course of study was stochastic systems, which required him to endlessly and fervently study in his Darden classes.

"I know what you mean, man," Anthony agreed. "As much as you stay shut up in that hole, you ought to be whizzin' on through," he commented further. Anthony had been watching Rossi for several weeks, studying his patterns and habits. With Rossi living above his head, it was easy for Anthony to determine when Rossi was home, in class, studying by music, or entertaining company. Many nights Anthony had stroked himself to sleep fantasizing about Rossi as he listened to the rhythmic squeaking and bumping of Rossi's bed over his head.

"I ain't tryna brag or nothing, but I'm pretty good with that if, you know, you want some help with it, man."

"Word?" Rossi questioned appreciatively.

"No doubt."

"Cool." Rossi slapped hands with Anthony again. "Good lookin' out, I'll get at you."

It wasn't long after that Rossi began climbing the steps

to the third floor to review notes and discuss lecture points, but several of their evenings ended in the two masturbating over porno films, with Anthony's eyes more focused on Rossi's exposed manhood than the lewd and explicit DVDs.

It was during one of these evenings that a drunken Rossi found himself with his head thrown back on Anthony's couch, eyes shut tight, enjoying the extreme pleasure of receiving oral sex from a chick that Anthony had invited over. He repeatedly thrust his hips forward as he pressed a mass of curly hair downward to meet him stroke for stroke. With a series of grunts he released his passion, then almost immediately fell asleep.

An hour later, though still asleep, he moaned in delight as he felt a set of soft lips and a warm mouth enclosed around his manhood. Slowly he peeled his eyes open to find Anthony knelt between his legs, and while his mind gasped in horror, his body betrayed him, unable to break away from the intensely gratifying sensation that pulsated through his very core. His uncontrolled groans fueled Anthony to plunge with increased momentum and vigor. When Rossi finally cried out, blurting a string of profane expressions, Anthony knew that Rossi would be back for more.

From that night up until Rossi graduated the following year, Jaison Anthony Mcdonald had given him several nights of indescribable pleasure.

For the next ten years, Rossi worked on convincing himself that he was not gay since the two had never engaged in intercourse, and the experience he'd shared with Anthony any woman could duplicate with some practice and a little coaching. Even during his involvement with Anthony, Rossi would close his eyes and pretend that Anthony was a female. And Anthony's long, wavy hair made it just a little bit easier to do.

* * *

After placing the letter on the counter, Rossi rifled through his kitchen drawer in search of matches. Not finding any, he resorted to using the front burner of his electric stove to ignite and destroy what would otherwise be incriminating evidence.

Turning the burner on high, he stood waiting for the coiled metal to glow red. Just as its darkened color began to change, the doorbell rang, drawing him away.

He padded to the door and peered through the peephole. "Who is it?" he huffed, not recognizing the man's face. He sighed in both relief and annoyance as Stephen announced himself. He'd forgotten all about his appointment that evening to have his property assessed so he and Micah could decide on a marital home. Before, he would have blown him off, but now in his commitment to marry Micah, he opened the door and welcomed Stephen.

"What's up, man? I forgot all about you coming over here this evening."

"How're you doing? You sure this is still a good time?" Stephen asked, meeting Rossi's hand with his own for a business shake.

"Yeah, it's cool. I'm a little tired, to be honest with you, but since you here, and I ain't 'sleep yet, we can go 'head and get this done. Come on in."

Stephen stepped into the foyer and took an initial glance around as he wiped his feet on the welcome mat just inside the door. "This is quite a home you have here."

"Thanks, man. I bought it as a foreclosure a few years back and fixed it up myself. I guess we can sit down in there"—he nodded his head toward the formal dining room—"so you can have some space to spread out whatever papers and stuff you'll need to show me." Rossi pushed the door closed and locked it while Stephen seated himself in the neighboring room. "All right, what you got for me?" Rossi asked, plopping down in a seat and rubbing a hand over his head.

"Why don't we start by you telling me a little bit about the house. Then, if you don't mind, walk me through it. I'll take some notes, then get back to you in a couple of days with a comparative market analysis. Then you and your fiancée can make a decision from there. I'm sure she shared with you that I was able to provide her with the same, which gave her some real numbers to consider."

"Cool. There're three bedrooms, two and a half bathrooms, living room, dining room, family room, fireplace. It was built in 1936, so it's pretty old, but, like I said, I've made some upgrades and renovations since I've had it. It has about twenty-five hundred square feet, a brick exterior, a detached garage out back." Rossi shrugged. "What else you need?"

"Are the floors hardwood throughout?" Stephen asked, turning his head to momentarily peer into the adjoining rooms.

"There's tile in the kitchen and carpet upstairs."

"I see you have crown molding." Stephen jotted a few notes on a legal pad. "That's nice."

"Yeah. Oh," Rossi remembered, "I've got a finished basement too."

"It's a pretty impressive property and probably wouldn't have any problem selling."

"How much you think I can get for it?"

"You probably have quite a bit of equity in it, but let's take a walk through first and let me jot down some other features."

"No doubt." Rossi bobbed his head as he pushed back in his chair and rose to his feet. The two men walked through the living room first as Rossi reached for his chiming cell phone.

"Hey, baby," Micah greeted.

"How's my baby doing?" Rossi replied.

"I'm fine. Just calling to check on you." Micah was taken aback by Rossi's unusual display of affectionate words.

"I miss you, babe. I can't wait to hold you in my arms again."

"Okay, what have you done with my fiancé? Either that or you must be drunk or something."

"No, baby, I'm just in love with you, that's all." He paused. Catching Rossi's attention, Stephen motioned if he could head toward the kitchen. Rossi nodded as he spoke to Micah, "The real estate guy is here looking at the house." Rossi trod behind Stephen.

"Okay, great! I was calling to see if he had made it over there, and to tell you that I'll be coming home next Sunday instead of this weekend so I can finish out the ramp-up."

"So you'll be out there for another week? Man! What are they doing, trying to hold my baby hostage?" He turned his attention to Stephen for a few seconds. "Excuse me, man, I'll be right back." Rossi headed down a short hallway and into the bathroom.

"Take your time." Stephen circled the kitchen making notes on his pad until his eyes came across the letter Rossi had left lying out on the granite countertop. Quickly his eyes scanned the

words as he listened for the flush of the toilet.
Stephen was shocked by what the letter revealed
and read over it a second time while Rossi continued his conversation with Micah in the bathroom. Finally hearing him turn on water to wash
his hands, Stephen quickly stepped toward the
double French doors that led to an expansive
deck and a backyard that measured more than
an acre. He tried to refocus his thoughts on his
job, but they were stuck on how he could tell
Micah that she was about to marry a no-good,
lying, cheating bastard. He strolled out into the
plush green grass that Rossi obviously took great
care to maintain. Somehow through his now
muddled thoughts, he managed to add to his list
of features that the property was beautifully
landscaped and enclosed by a privacy fence.
Hearing the sound of the French doors closing
behind him, Stephen turned to look over his
shoulder. "You have a really nice yard, man," he
commented.

Rossi folded his arms across his chest, proud of
his yard. "I tried to convince my fiancée to get married right out here, but she ain't tryna hear it."

"Outdoor weddings are always nice," Stephen
forced from his lips, although there were quite a
few other choice words he would have rather said.
"When I find the right woman, we might have to
come here and tie the knot," he joked.

"Just let me know, man. I'll rent you some time
out here. Would let you get it for free, but uh, I'm
'bout to take a wife." Rossi chuckled. "I'ma need
some extra cash."

"I heard that. Can we take a look upstairs?"
Stephen suggested, now trying to speed up the
process.

The men walked back into the kitchen, where Rossi noticed the eye of the stove glowing red. His eyes glanced over to the countertop where he'd left the letter as he stepped toward the stove and turned the knob to "off." Quickly he flipped the document over, then led the way to the stairwell, hoping that Stephen hadn't noticed it.

Another thirty minutes passed before Stephen wrapped up his visit, promising to get back with Rossi in a few days.

"All right, man," Rossi extended his hand once more as he opened his door to let Stephen out. "I'll look to hear from you soon," he added, stepping out onto the front porch.

"Is that your truck?" Stephen nodded his head toward the Expedition parked on the street.

"Yeah." He nodded.

"Looks like you've got a flat."

"What the . . ." Rossi bounded down the porch steps and across the yard to his vehicle. His first thought was that it had been an act of spiteful revenge, considering the letter he'd received, but upon closer inspection, he realized that he'd inadvertently driven over the shank of a screwdriver. "Man, if it ain't one thing, it's another," he huffed, then cursed.

"That's how it always is. I'll call you, man." Stephen settled into his two-seater Mercedes and pulled off, leaving Rossi digging the jack out of the trunk of his car.

This time when Rossi went in the house, he headed straight for the shower and then only meant to sit on the bed, but before he knew it, he was out like a light.

The next morning he shot up in bed like a rocket, instantly reminded of Jaison's letter.

Right away, he jogged down to his kitchen; turned the stove on; lit the corner of the letter; and watched the paper crinkle, blacken, and dissolve in his kitchen sink. Turning on the faucet, he washed the ashes down the drain, then let out a heavy sigh.

You've Been Approved!

After answering a string of e-mails and making some personal notes for herself, Micah shut her laptop down, tucked it under the seat in front of her, and leaned her head on the window. She smiled to herself as she thought back on her trip. The site ramp had been successful, she'd been able to complete her postvisit assessment reports the previous evening, and she'd gotten the face time with Gerald Stone that she'd needed to gain some leverage on her next career move. If she played her cards right, a smooth transition and a very nice salary increase would be in her near future.

The plane glided downward until it smoothly met the runway. Before the flight attendant could give the official approval, Micah, along with the other passengers, reached for their pocketbooks or carry-ons and began using their cell phones. Out of habit, Micah let out a sigh, hoping that for once in her life Rossi would be on time. He'd arrived back home more than a week earlier but had agreed to pick her up from the airport. With quick fingers, she sent a text message notifying him of her arrival. Seven more minutes passed between the plane taxiing to the gate and her actually stepping into the terminal, with no response from Rossi. She concluded that she'd just take a cab home, not having the patience to wait for Rossi. After being on the road for more than a month, there was nothing she wanted more than to sit in her own bathtub and sleep in her own bed.

As she rounded the corner of the hallway and headed for the ground transportation exit, she was floored by what she saw. Fully suited in a tuxedo, Rossi was already positioned on one knee centered in the airport's atrium with three dozen long-stemmed red roses cradled in his left arm and a dazzling three-carat diamond ring in his right.

Completely stunned, Micah stopped in her tracks and covered her mouth with both hands. Her luggage fell over to the side, causing a rushing traveler to nearly trip, but instead of yelling obscenities, he mumbled a quick congratulations as he leapt over her bag and continued his stride.

"Oh, sorry. Thanks," she replied sheepishly as she gathered her things, then strolled to Rossi with a smile that just couldn't help but spread wide across her face.

"Micah, I love you, baby."

"Rossi I . . ."

"Babe, let me finish." With soulful eyes filling with water, he continued, "I know that I haven't always done right by you. So many times I've taken you for granted and didn't treat you like the queen you are. I know that right now I don't even deserve you, but if you would just give me one more opportunity, I promise I will put you on a pedestal and worship the very ground you walk on. Micah, please accept this ring, just a mere symbol and very small token of the love that I truly have for you. I've fallen short before, but today, I'm humbled at your feet as I ask you, Micah Paris Abraham, to become Mrs. Rossi Jerome Evans." He finished as he reached for her hand and slid the ring onto the appropriate finger. "Will you marry me, Micah?"

"When, Rossi?" she blurted in bliss accompanied by a bit of anger and disbelief.

"Baby, whenever you say. Whichever day you choose to do me the honor of becoming my wife."

Micah's thoughts were a blur as she remembered in an instant every time Rossi had stood her up, disregarded her feelings, and put her last on his list of important things. In the next instant, all of those things flew out the window; nothing else seemed to matter. Rossi wanted to marry her, and this time he had the ring to prove it.

By this time a small crowd had gathered to hear Micah's response. She thought about the many times she'd been stood up, the save-the-date e-mail that had to be recalled, how ashamed he seemed to be of her, the humiliation she felt at his family reunion. She thought about how many times she'd been introduced as his "friend" and how unfulfilled she was in their relationship. Kaycee's warning rushed its way to the forefront of her memories. The thoughts swirled wildly in her head as she looked into Rossi's eyes, which radiated with sincerity as he awaited her answer. He circled her palm with his thumb and licked his bottom lip.

"Will you marry me, Micah?"

Micah bobbed her head slightly as she whispered, "Yes . . . yes, baby." Onlookers clapped and cheered as Rossi rose to his feet, gathered Micah in his arms, and kissed her as tenderly as if it were the first time, then ended with a kiss as fiery as the last time they'd made passionate love.

Let's Take Our Time

Rossi and Micah stretched out on his living room sofa watching a BET movie. For the first time in a long time, he was completely elated and fulfilled. He pressed his lips atop Micah's head and tightened his arms around her. His mind momentarily drifted away from the movie as he thought about how fortunate he was to have Micah in his life . . . still.

"Baby," he spoke softly.

"Hmm?"

"I love you."

"I love you too, babe," she responded without thought.

Rossi's thoughts drifted to Micah's vision for their wedding. She wanted everybody she knew and had ever known to be there and had more than doubled their original estimation of 150 guests. Every day she shared with him a new wedding idea: exquisite flowers, unique favors, elaborate decorations. Each time, he bit his tongue, not wanting her to get the impression that he was

trying to back out, but he knew what she expressed would cost thousands of dollars, which
was money he simply didn't have. There were a
couple of options at his disposal, including refi-
nancing his home, getting a line of equity or a
second job, or opening new credit accounts.
None of those things sounded like good ideas to
him. He would much rather have a simple ceremony with just a few witnesses; no fanfare and
fluff. At the end of the day, it seemed to be such
a waste of money. Even an exchange of vows at
the local Justice of the Peace would be enough
for him, and it would allow him to pour more
money into their honeymoon. He wished for
something out of the ordinary, something neither
one of them would forget for a very long time.
The Bahamas, Hawaii, and Cancun all seemed
typical, not to mention he'd been there before
with former lovers and wanted to share a location
that would be exclusive to the both of them. He'd
begun researching a few other locations to include Australia and Fiji. For what Micah wanted
to spend on the wedding, he could book them a
two-week stay on a remote island. Nonetheless, it
would be her day and he was willing to give her
the world regardless of the cost.

As the closing credits scrolled up the screen,
Rossi began planting kisses on Micah's shoulders.
"Mmm," he moaned as he pressed his hips forward into her behind. "I love you," he whispered.
"And I can't wait to make you my wife." She
turned her body toward him and returned his af-
fections. "I'm going to make love to you every"—
he paused to press his lips against her
flesh—"single . . . night." His hands slid up her
body and began to caress her breasts as he bit into

his bottom lip and looked into her eyes. In sudden passionate aggression, their lips connected in a furious and wet kiss.

Rossi began to lift up from the couch to lead Micah to the bedroom, but she pulled back hesitantly. "Baby, wait," she said softly.

"What's wrong, babe? It's that time of the month?" he asked, not slowing his kisses.

"No." She pecked his lips before she continued. "No, it's not that but . . ." She paused pensively. "Rossi, I want our wedding night to be special."

"Okay?" he responded, coaxing her to continue. "It will be. I guarantee that," he said, maneuvering her hand to his manhood, wanting her to stroke him.

"Seriously, Rossi," she said, giving his stiffening body an adoring squeeze. "I want it to be special and not like what we're used to already doing."

"So what are you saying, baby?" Rossi questioned, although he had a strong feeling as to what Micah was getting at.

"I love you, but I don't want to make love again until we get married." She looked into Rossi's eyes for a response. "I know the wedding is a ways off, but it would mean a lot to me to wait."

"Wait for what, baby? We've already made love a thousand times. I mean, what is waiting gonna do?" Rossi countered. "You want me to let go of all this?" he asked, reaching down to squeeze both halves of her behind.

"Just for a little while, baby," she whined. "I want it to be like the first time all over again."

Rossi blew out a puff of air. "Micah, come on, baby. You're asking me to be celibate for six whole months?" He tossed his head back and stared up at the ceiling knowing that if he didn't agree,

Micah would suggest that their relationship was built only on sex. At the same time, he wasn't looking forward to spending nights in bed alone with his sexual needs unfulfilled.

"Please, baby. It would really mean a lot to me. I know we can't go back and pretend to have never experienced each other, and I love the way you make love to me, but I want to be able to look forward to making love to you that night." She reached behind her and grasped Rossi's hands, then pulled them away from her butt.

"Micah, I look forward to making love to you every time I'm with you. It's always special to me," he responded, resting his forehead against hers. "That's not going to change."

"I'm not saying that it will, Rossi; I just want to wait. I want to have that feeling of being anxious to leave the reception, instead of partying all night because we've become so familiar with each other, it's just the norm. I want to learn you all over again, baby, and feel you for the first time all over again," she said, nearly pleading.

Rossi knew there was nothing else he could do but agree. "Okay," he sighed. "Just let me have you one more time, baby," he requested, pulling her closer.

"Rossi," she said firmly.

"All right, all right. I just thought I'd try." He lovingly kissed her cheek, then her lips. "I will do my best to hold out, baby, but I can't promise you that I won't try you." His hands slid to her rounded backside again as he pressed his manhood forward. "You know you're irresistible," he murmured. He kissed her passionately once more, hoping to charm her to his bedroom, yet Micah resisted.

"I guess I'd better go home," she suggested as she slowly pulled away.

"Yeah. You might be right, because if you hang around here much longer, we're not going to make it through the night."

Micah turned her back to Rossi and nestled into his arms as they trudged through his front door and to her car, him nibbling on her neck along the way.

"Six months, huh?"

"It will fly by," she said encouragingly, taking a seat in her car and letting the window down.

Rossi heaved a sigh. "All right, babe." He stuck his head inside the window and pecked her lips. "Call me when you get home."

"I will," Micah promised. "I love you."

"I love you, baby." Slowly she pulled out of Rossi's driveway, feeling more excited about her engagement than she ever had.

Rossi stood in place watching as she drove to the corner and then made a right turn out of his subdivision. "Six months," he said to himself, chuckling, then shook his head. "A whole half a year. Lord, give me strength."

Just a Few Questions

"You look beautiful, baby," Rossi commented as he opened the passenger door of his car to let Micah out. She stepped onto the pavement dressed in a silky royal blue halter dress trimmed in lime green. A few jeweled hairpins kept her soft curls out of her eyes but allowed them to gently frame her face. A chic pair of blue and lime open-toe, wedge-heeled platforms added four inches to her height.

Once she stood, she pecked Rossi on the lips. "Thank you, baby." She blushed.

He wrapped his arm around her waist, pushed the door closed, and slipped his hand into hers. "I love you," he whispered in her ear.

"Do you?" She grinned at Rossi and leaned into his shoulder.

"Absolutely." He lifted her hand to his lips, kissed it, then stared at her ring with a smile as they started to walk. Together they entered an office building, took the elevator to the seventh floor, and found suite 7209.

"We have an appointment with Mrs. Smith," Rossi spoke to the receptionist.

"Sure. I'll let her know you're here," she replied, then moments later led them down a hallway to a counseling lounge. "Can I get you anything to drink?" she offered.

"I'll take a Sprite or 7-Up if you have that," Micah requested.

"How about a Sierra Mist?"

"That will be fine."

"I'll just have some room-temperature water please," Rossi added.

"No problem. Mrs. Smith will be with you shortly."

Just as the young lady appeared at the room's entrance with their beverages, Sonya Smith entered from an alternate door.

"Mr. Evans and Ms. Abraham," she greeted warmly as she extended her hand. Impeccably dressed in a black Anne Klein notched-collar, wide-legged pantsuit, accompanied by a turquoise shell and jewelry, she commanded attention and respect. Rossi stood respectfully to meet her hand, while Micah remained seated. "It's a pleasure to meet you both," she said, flashing a set of beautifully straight teeth. "So you want to get married, huh?" She sat in a single chair across from the couple and beamed professionally as she took note of their body language. Micah sat with her legs crossed dangling her foot at Rossi's shin and leaning into him slightly. Rossi sat relaxed back into the loveseat's cushion with his knees and feet apart cupping Micah's left hand in his right and holding it at his chest.

"Yes, we do." Rossi grinned, then puckered his lips to meet Micah's cheek. "This is my baby right here," he said, patting her knee.

"You two look adorable," Sonya complimented, smiling as she spoke. "Marriage is a beautiful thing; it's also a very serious decision and a step that's not to be entered into flippantly." Sonya's tone transitioned from professionally pleasant to firm and resolute. "I'm going to tell you, it takes hard work and determination to make a marriage successful." Micah's eyes caught sight of the exquisite wedding rings on Sonya's hand, which was clasped with the other and resting on her lap. "I'm elated to see that you two are not taking the consideration of your union lightly in that you're seeking counseling prior to the wedding. I believe more marriages, thus lives, could be saved if couples realized the value and importance of premarital counseling, as well as postcounseling, when necessary." She paused momentarily to look pensively at both Micah and Rossi, communicating her conviction and belief in the intensity of her stare. "Do either of you come from two-parent homes?"

Micah started first. "I was actually raised in the foster care system and lived in a number of homes until I was about fourteen. Then I was able to go live with a female cousin who was about twenty at the time," she shared.

"I was raised solely by my mother," Rossi spoke. "My dad was killed in the streets of Atlanta shortly after my twin sister and I were born."

Sonya nodded, then continued, "Tell me how the two of you met."

"She actually came in my restaurant to eat and asked for the manager, which would be me, to complain that her food wasn't hot enough, her tea wasn't sweet enough, and the service wasn't fast enough." Rossi chuckled. "It took a little work to calm her down, and I had to comp her meal, but hey, it all worked out . . . for my good, I might add."

"Love at first sight?" she asked next. They both blushed.

"I'm scared to say love. How about very strong like at first site?" Micah quipped, with a giggle.

"I see, so that's a yes." Sonya laughed before addressing Rossi. "And, Rossi, what about you? When did you realize that you were in love with Micah?"

Rossi spent the next several seconds thinking, then trying to communicate Micah's sentiments, but could not. "I can't pinpoint exactly where and when I fell in love with her, but all I know is I'm in love with her now."

"Every relationship starts somewhere, so there is nothing wrong with that. So we're going to begin with some questions that you really need to be able to answer about each other. Some you may be able to answer right away, and others you may need to think about a bit before you respond, which is okay too," she said, handing each of them a pad and a pen. "You may want to jot the questions and/or your answers down. Now I would encourage you to share freely in this session." The couple nodded, then Sonya read off her first question. "Rossi, what have you learned to appreciate about Micah that you didn't know when you two first became a couple?"

Rossi thought pensively for several seconds, then began speaking. "I didn't realize how sensitive and caring Micah was when I met her." He turned his head to look directly into Micah's eyes. "She is so very understanding and forgiving . . . even though I've taken her for granted more times than I'd like to admit."

"And what about you, Micah?"

Micah chose her words carefully. The past month or so had been wonderful, even without the presence of sex, but Micah still had her reservations about Rossi's love for her. "Well, one of the things that I've learned and most appreciate about Rossi is the love he has for his family, more specifically the women in his life. I have seen the way he loves and adores his mother, and how protective he is of his twin sister. That gives me the assurance that I need to know that he will always treat me well as his wife," she managed in pure honesty.

"And that is a great sign. How a man treats his mother is a great indicator of what you can expect of him as a husband." Sonya nodded. "Let's move on to the next question. Micah, I'll start with you. What have you learned about Rossi that irritates, upsets, or frightens you?"

Micah jotted the question down on her pad before she parted her lips to answer. "Rossi doesn't always keep his word," Micah began, thinking of the many times she'd been stood up or let down by her fiancé. "It irritates me because it makes me feel like I'm not important to him, but I can say that I see him growing in that area. There still has to be a little trust built in that area for me," Micah admitted.

"She's right," Rossi interjected. "I have messed up quite a few times, but, like I said, Micah's been so forgiving." He rested his hand on her thigh and lovingly squeezed it. "And, Micah, I want to say to you that I am totally committed to working on that. I *will* earn your trust," he finished.

Sonya again gave an approving nod, then asked Rossi to answer the same question. "What irritates me a little about Micah is I think sometimes she is way too independent, so she will do something like make a decision without talking to me first, or waiting for me to give an answer. That makes me feel like she doesn't have a need for me, you know?" he responded. "I know she is capable of taking care of herself, but I also want to know that she needs me on some level."

"Do you need him, Micah?"

Micah scratched her head before she answered. "Honestly, I think I want to need him, but this goes back to him working on keeping his word. If he can't keep his word, then he forces me to not need him," she tried to explain. "For example, if I mention that I need to have the oil changed in my car, he might offer to take it for me, but when he doesn't do it, I'm forced to do it myself. I would much rather that he do it, so yes, I need him, but when he doesn't follow through and I have to do it myself, then no, I don't need him."

"She makes a great point, Rossi. What you need to ask yourself is, as your wife, can Micah depend on you?"

"Yes, she can," Rossi said without delay.

"Tell her that."

"Micah, you can depend on me. I want to do for you; I want to provide for you; I want to take care of you, baby. I need you to need me." He bit his bottom lip and cleared his throat to maintain his composure, then kept silent.

"Micah, are you satisfied with the amount of time the two of you spend together?" Sonya asked.

"Yes and no," Micah started after a few seconds of contemplation. "We both have pretty demanding jobs and usually work fifty to sixty hours a week. I think the both of us are very aware and considerate of that, so we try not to be too demanding, but there are times that we both are free and I want to be with him and he'll have something to do," Micah said as she remembered how Rossi had taken three days off from work to spend with his sister during the week she'd visited. Of that seventy-two-hour time frame, he'd given Micah less than ten minutes.

"How about you, Rossi?" Sonya asked, turning her head toward him.

"She's right about what she just said. I find myself missing her when I can't see her. A lot of times we can't sync our schedules, but you know what they say"—he chuckled—"absence makes the heart grow fonder."

"I think you answered the next question already, but I'll share it with you just in case you want to put it in your notes," Sonya quipped, having noticed Micah recording both the questions and portions of Rossi's responses. "Are you pleased with the amount of time you spend apart?" Sonya paused briefly to allow either of them to respond. They both looked at each other as they spent a few seconds in thought, then concluded that they'd addressed the matter already. Sonya continued, "Rossi, what have you given up for Micah?"

There was an uncomfortable period of silence while Rossi's eyes scanned the room, his gaze landing on random objects. Micah bit into her bottom lip as she tried to recall sacrifices Rossi had made for her sake. Unfortunately, she couldn't think of a single thing. She kept silent as Rossi seemed to be lost in his thoughts. Finally, with a slight nod, he said generically, "I think in getting married, we both will give up our freedom and selfishness."

"Micah?" Sonya directed.

"I've turned down a few job opportunities for

the sake of our relationship. Of course, those jobs came with a higher salary, so indirectly I've sacrificed money." This time Micah's gaze shifted around the room. "I've given time. Sometimes it was wasted when it could have been used on other things." She shrugged. *Keep your cool, Micah,* she coached, feeling herself becoming a bit irritated. "I'll stop there for the purpose of time," she ended as she thought of a few other things but decided it was better to keep them to herself.

"How do you feel about those things, Micah? The job, the potential income, your time . . ." Sonya circled with her hand to indicate a longer list.

Micah's response was led by a thoughtful sigh. "I obviously feel that Rossi meant more to me than whatever I gave up, or else I would have decided differently." She nodded with confidence, then smiled at her fiancé. "I think what God has for me is for me, so believing that He has all things in control, I'm sure that I'm right where I'm supposed to be."

"See. That's why I have to marry this woman," Rossi boasted. "She's incredible."

"I'm glad you recognize her value," Sonya responded. "I have one more question for the two of you and then we will be out of time," she said, glancing at her watch. "At what times have you felt happiest together?"

"Every moment that I've been with her," Rossi began. He continued for another five minutes giving examples of times and situations in which he felt the two of them were at their best.

On the other hand, Micah couldn't think of a time when Rossi had sincerely made her happy for longer than a day or two.

* * *

The ride back home was silent as Micah was lost in her thoughts about the questions Sonya had presented and her responses. Rossi's hand rested on her knee as he intermittently looked over and smiled at her.

"I love you, baby," he murmured lovingly.

Micah smiled back. "I love you too." As they slowed to a stop at a traffic light, he leaned over and kissed her lips lightly. "I'm a lucky man."

Later that night, Micah revisited every question that had been asked in the counseling session forcing herself to be completely honest. Cracking the seal of a new journal, she wrote pages and pages of her thoughts, feeling, and emotions. Nearly three hours passed as she reflected on her relationship and why she wanted to be Mrs. Rossi Jerome Evans.

"Follow your heart," she whispered to herself. Now mentally exhausted, she put her pen down, knowing she was making the right decision.

Final Fitting

Six months later . . .

Erin examined her body after she stepped from the shower and slathered on a layer of baby oil. She smiled as she admired her new figure. After that fateful date at her Ob/Gyn's office, she'd made herself a promise: To thine ownself be true.

Over the past several months, Erin had made a complete turnaround in every facet of her life. She'd never forgotten the health seminar that she'd attended shortly after her visit to Dr. Corbin's office.

"Your body needs life to live," the speaker had commented. In his opening, he'd shared with the audience that twenty years prior he had been diagnosed with cancer and given an estimated six months to live. "I just couldn't accept that," he had said into the microphone. "My kids were young, my wife was beautiful, and I hadn't accomplished much of anything besides graduating from college. That wasn't how I wanted my life to end. I took it upon myself to make some changes. I took it upon myself to study God's word and seek Him on what I should do. His word says He heals us of *all* our diseases, so I knew there was something in His word for me."

Erin had sat on the edge of her seat with her pen poised to capture every word.

"God created our bodies so that they are self-healing," the speaker had continued. "If you cut your hand, after some time it scabs over and heals. But when your body is not properly nourished, it's not equipped to repair itself. In order to do that, you have to feed your body life—you do that by giving your body live foods, or foods that have not been destroyed by heat. When you cook your vegetables, you kill the life that's in them.

"Think of it like this. If you cut open an apple, remove the seeds, and plant them, what happens? They grow, right?" His audience nodded. "Now, if you take that same apple, remove the seeds and boil them in a pot of water, then plant them, what do you think will happen? Nothing, because there is no longer any life in those seeds. When you eat raw fruits and vegetables, you are feeding your body life, and you equip your body with what it needs to properly heal and repair itself. You see, your body can deal with only a certain amount of abuse. Sugars, fats, and processed foods don't contain life. After a while, those sugars, fats, and processed foods turn into high blood pressure, heart disease, cancer, ulcers, headaches, and all kinds of ailments. Those foods are dead, and death does not beget life. Life begets life."

The speaker went on for another hour or so answering questions about what he recommended for healthy eating and sharing natural remedies

for various physical complaints. Once the seminar
came to an end, Erin headed for the mall in
search of a juicer because the speaker recommended drinking freshly made juices every day.
Settling on the Jack LaLanne, having seen his in-
fomercial on TV a few times, she paid the cashier,
then picked up a plethora of fresh fruits and vegetables from the grocery store, committing to con-
sistently using her new appliance.

Now, months later, Erin couldn't have been
more pleased with the outcome. Her most recent
doctor's visits had revealed normal Pap smears
with no sign of cancerous cells, and she had easily
lost more than sixty pounds. She sauntered from
the bathroom and slipped into a size eight jogging
suit, still unable to believe that she no longer wore
a size twenty.

Smiling to herself, she was proud of the new
woman she'd become—cancer, extra weight, and
Gideon free. Despite his frequent phone calls,
e-mails, and text messages, she hadn't spoken a
single word with him since she had been diagnosed
with HPV. And she couldn't have been happier.

On her way to her car, she dialed Micah's
number. "Are you ready?"

"Yeah, just waiting on you," she sang just before
biting into a bagel. "I'm supposed to be there at
eleven, so I hope you're on your way."

"I'm leaving my house right now. We should get
there in plenty of time. Have you talked to Victori and Charvette?"

"They are both here already, going over the
final details of the rehearsal dinner."

"Cool. I can't believe you are almost a married woman." Erin giggled. "I'll see you in a few
minutes."

Within thirty minutes the four ladies pulled into the parking lot of the bridal shop and entered full of giggles from reminiscing about old times during the car ride, but they quickly quieted themselves. Micah's consultant retrieved her gown from the back and handed it to her, and then Micah disappeared into a dressing room.

"One of these days, this is going to be me. Call me when she comes out," Charvette said, wandering off to view wedding gowns.

"I'm never getting married," Victori commented. "It's just too many hot boys out there for me." She settled back in a chair and pulled a magazine out of her purse. "Plus, I ain't met a man yet who comes with the total package—the looks, the tools and the skills to use them, plus the extra attachments and accessories," she continued. "This one can use the hips but don't know how to use the lips. That one's big and strong but usually don't last too long. And if one know how to lick, he can't work the stick."

"What did you do, go to a rap class before you came here?" Erin asked, rising from her seat, clearly irritated by Victori's blunt sharing. "Micah, do you need any help?" she asked, tapping on the dressing room door. Just as she did, Micah emerged in an elegant Paloma Blanca strapless gown embellished with sparkling crystal beads that formed various swirls and spirals. Satin-covered buttons trailed from the small of her back down to the hem of the dress's full train. She stepped onto the elevated platform surrounded by four large mirrors and admired her reflection as she turned from side to side.

"It is absolutely stunning," Erin commented, backed by Victori. Micah could only clasp her hands over her mouth, astounded by her own beauty.

Victori and Erin stooped at her feet to arrange her train after tugging at the lining to remove a few wrinkles visible beneath a layer of chiffon. "Girl, Rossi is going to flip when he sees you in this," Erin spoke, gathering Micah's hair into her fist and twisting it into a mock updo. She studied Micah's facial structure in the mirror. "Are you going to wear your hair up?"

"I think so, as long as it can be soft. I want my husband to be able to run his fingers through it that night, not feel like he's patting on a turtle-shell."

"How long has it been again since you two did it?" Victori asked bluntly.

"You are so nosy!" Erin chastised.

"Months," Micah whispered, still mesmerized with her mirrored image.

"I don't see how you can do it, girl." Victori collapsed back into her seat. "You're better than me. I can't wait for nothing." She giggled.

Micah shook her head. "There's more to life than sex, Victori."

"Like what? I got my own car, job, house, and money." She shrugged as her volume grew progressively louder. "Can't a man do nothing for me besides give me some good . . ."

"Will you shut up!" Erin said through clenched teeth, glancing around at other customers in the store. "We can't take you anywhere. Act like you got some sense," she said, slapping Victori on the arm.

"Oh, I got good sense," Victori shot back, lowering her tone. "I just don't always use it." The three women laughed together.

"Well, this is it ladies." Micah finally pulled away from the mirror and turned toward her friends. "A week from now it will be a done deal."

"So what are you doing with your little black book?" Victori piped up again.

"Will you give it a rest? I don't even have a little black book." Micah threw up her arms.

"Well, just give me that real estate guy's number. That will do."

"No! You already got a house, remember?"

"It's not a house I'm after."

"Why did we bring her again? Unzip this dress for me please," Micah said, turning her back to Erin. Moments later she was back in the privacy of the dressing room thinking about her soon approaching wedding date.

As if he were reading her mind, Rossi's number appeared on her cell phone screen accompanied by a "Here Comes the Bride" ringtone. Wriggling out of her clothes, she flipped her phone open.

"Hey."

"How're you doing, sweetie?" Rossi asked.

"Good. Just picking up my gown," she shared.

"I can't wait to see you in it."

"And I can't wait to marry you." She heard the smile in his voice as he spoke his next words.

"I was just calling to let you know that I'm on my way to the airport to pick up my mom. You still are going to be able to make it to dinner tomorrow night, right?" Rossi had planned to prepare his special baked chicken, which was his mom's favorite.

"Of course, Rossi. I wouldn't miss it for the world," Micah answered as she carefully hung the gown up and zipped it in its bag.

"Momma's looking forward to seeing you again."

"She said that?" Micah asked with surprise.

"Yeah. She's excited about the wedding and the hope of having some grandbabies."

"Oh brother!" Giggles escaped Micah's lips as she pulled her jeans over her hips. "She wants you to keep me barefoot and pregnant, huh?"

"You know we're from the country, baby," Rossi answered, chuckling. "I'm here at the airport now, so I'll call you back in a little while."

"Okay, sounds good."

"I love you, Micah."

"Love you too," she blurted. She exited the dressing room with a smile on her face. "You ladies ready? I think I'm all done here."

"What are you grinnin' about?" Victori asked.

"Just got off the phone with my man."

Victori rolled her eyes. "I should have known."

"Don't hate. You know you're looking for love," Micah retorted.

"Nope, I'm just looking for lust."

"And that's gonna catch up with you sooner or later," Erin warned. She had never shared her situation with anyone other than Micah.

"And when it does, I'll probably be sick of running anyway."

"Where's Charvette?" Micah asked on her way to the customer service counter to sign off on her alterations.

"Over there looking at gowns. I'll get her." Victori darted off into a row filled with white, bagged garments.

"So you're actually going to do it, huh?" Erin asked.

Micah only smiled at her friend.

"I'm so happy for you." Erin tossed an arm around Micah's shoulders. "I know it's been a rocky road."

"I just wish I had your figure, girl! I should have been drinking juice right along with you."

"You look great, Micah. And your gown is beautiful. It's so wonderful that you have someone to wear it for."

Micah stopped in her tracks, pressed her lips together, and stared at Erin. "What's wrong?" Micah stood silent for a few more seconds until she saw Victori and Charvette approaching. "We have to talk," she whispered.

"When?" Erin looked confused, anxious, and worried.

"Later," Micah answered careful not to move her lips.

"Can we go eat now, Ms. Princess Queen?" Victori asked. "I'm starving."

"Yep. Let's go," Erin answered while Micah jetted to the counter to complete the paperwork for her gown pickup.

When Micah spun toward her friends, a half smile crossed her face. She gathered the gown in her arms as tears gathered in her eyes. "Do y'all realize that this is the last time we'll go out together as unmarried girlfriends?" She focused on each of their faces, then shrieked through her tears, "Group hug!" The ladies circled around her and enveloped each other in their arms. "Because next week, I won't have time for none of y'all!" The quad broke out in laughter and headed for the car.

"Now what's going on with you?" Erin asked, propping her feet up on Micah's coffee table after Micah saw the other two ladies out.

Micah sighed and took a seat beside her friend. She pressed her lips together again as she struggled with her thoughts. "Promise me that this will stay between us."

"Come on, Micah, you know that goes without saying."

"I know but it feels better to say it than to not say it." Micah tilted her head back and closed her eyes.

"Well, of course you have my word that what's said in this room stays in this room."

"I told you Rossi and I completed counseling, right?"

"Yeah." Erin stood and walked to the kitchen to get some water. "You want anything out of here while I'm up?"

"Just some ice."

When Erin returned, Micah continued. "Okay, so I have been tracking and journalizing the questions that were asked in our counseling sessions. And counseling has been awesome; it's really made me open my eyes and think about some things. I've been coming home and studying the questions and our answers, and even answering them more in-depth once I've had a chance to think more about them." She reached for her cup of ice but Erin stopped her.

"Girl, please don't start eating that now. You're going to start slurring and slurping. Can we finish talking first?"

"You're lucky you're my maid of honor," Micah responded, placing the cup back on the table.

"So what is it—you're getting cold feet?" Erin asked with concern. "Or are you having doubts?"

"No, no. It's not that." She shook her head rapidly. "I'm more certain about what I'm doing than anything I've ever done before in my whole life. I

know what I'm doing is the right thing for me."
Micah stared blankly at the wall in front of her.

"Okay? So . . ." Erin circled her hands encouraging Micah to continue toward her point.

"I don't want you to think less of me," Micah said, tussling with her confession.

"You don't love him, do you?"

"What?" Micah instantly shot. "What makes you say a thing like that, Erin?" Her crinkled brows expressed offense.

"Well, what is it? You cheated on him?" she asked, with wide-stretched eyes.

"Will you calm down! No, I haven't cheated on him. But . . ." She rose to her feet and began to pace the floor, then shook her head. "I can't tell you." She collapsed on her chaise. "You'll have to wait until the wedding."

"You're pregnant and the two of you will make an announcement at the reception," Erin guessed. Micah smiled in response. "Oh my goodness! I'm going to be an auntie? How far are you? What did Rossi say?"

"I haven't told Rossi."

"What? Why?"

Micah shrugged.

"Micah, how are you going to marry this man and not be able to tell him before the wedding that you're carrying his child? That is great news!"

"What's so great about it? Rossi said he wasn't ready to have kids yet. Remember?"

"That was before he officially, officially proposed," Erin replied. "But things have really taken off in the right direction and have been going really well for the two of you."

"You think so?"

"You don't think so, Micah? That man has love

oozing out of his pores right now, and would do anything for you. Now I've got to admit, I couldn't say this last year, or even six months ago, but now? Rossi is crazy about you. He'd probably be elated about a baby."

"I'm glad you think so."

"And you don't?" Erin paused as she studied Micah's solemn expression. "I don't think you should tell him at the same time that you announce it to the world, though."

"Well I didn't say that; you did."

"So when are you going to tell him?"

"Maybe after dinner tomorrow night. Just promise me you won't say anything about this before the wedding."

"Wait a minute," Erin snapped. "I thought you were holding out on sex until the wedding night."

Micah shrugged with a smirk. "What can I say?"

"You must be so excited," Erin gushed.

"I have mixed feelings actually," Micah said in a tone less than jubilant.

"You'll be just fine," Erin consoled.

I Now Pronounce
You Mr. and Mrs. . . .

Before she knew it, Micah's alarm clock buzzed,
arousing her for the day. Excited yet exhausted,
she dragged herself to the bathroom, assessed in
the mirror the damages of staying up too late, and
reasoned that it was nothing a few ice cubes
couldn't fix. Strength came once she got in the
shower and covered her face with Noxema. The
menthol opened her eyes right up and gave Micah
the energy she needed to pull it together for her
big day.

She had about an hour to get down to the
church for hair and make-up. Charvette, who had
recovered remarkably well from her injuries,
would style Micah's hair in spiraled tendrils, and
Erin, who had recently found success as a Mary
Kay consultant, would do her make-up. Shortly
after, Micah was scheduled to zip up into her
$3,000 gown and take the walk of her life.

The hallway echoed with emptiness as Micah

took steps toward the door to let Erin in. Micah had successfully moved, sold, or put into storage everything she owned and had her home painted in preparation for the renter who would occupy the property by month's end.

"Hey, the-very-soon-to-be Mrs. Evans," Erin chimed, grabbing Micah in a tight hug. "So how are you feeling, honey? Are you nervous?"

"Just a little, but I'm ready. I've waited for this day for so long and it's finally here!" she squealed.

"Yeah, he took long enough, but your time has come." Erin leaned against the front wall since there was nowhere to sit.

"Let me grab my purse and say good-bye to my walls one last time," Micah said, then darted to the kitchen first, then back down the hallway to her bedroom for the last time.

"Girl, you don't have time to be talking to the walls. Come on here. We need to roll," Erin chastised, charging down the hall and grabbing Micah by her arm before she reached the bedroom.

"All right! I'm coming."

After locking the door for the last time, Micah handed Erin the house keys for her to pass on to the realty management company.

"I thought you were going to ride with me?" Erin questioned as Micah unarmed her truck and slid into the driver's seat.

"Well, I was, but I changed my mind. Somebody might need to run out and get something for me and you know you're not going to let them use your truck. Plus, I don't feel like digging all my luggage out of here and transferring it to your truck just to put it in Rossi's truck when we get to the church."

"So I just wasted my gas coming over here then. Is that what you telling me?"

"I'm sorry, girl. I should have called you. But you know you wanted to see me early on my last day of singleness anyway."

"Yeah, right. I could have slept another hour," she dismissed, with a wave of her hand. "You are so lucky I love you."

"And I love you too, so let's go. I'm hungry."

Erin backed out, then waited for Micah to pull out of the driveway, and they both drove to Starbucks for coffee and bagels. On the way, Micah snatched the greasy scarf off of her head and finger combed her locks out of their nighttime wrap. Before she got out the vehicle, she checked her glove compartment for the plane tickets that she knew were there. She just had to lay eyes on them one more time. Yep. There they were. Perfect.

"You look incredible!" Victori gasped as she shook her head slowly from side to side, smiling. "I've never seen a more beautiful bride."

"I don't even have my dress on yet, Victori."

"So you're just going to look that much more stunning once you get in it."

Micah blushed as she tightened a towel around her chest. "Thanks."

"And don't move out of that chair until those toenails dry," Victori ordered, packing up her nail kit.

"Actually, if you ladies don't mind, I need to spend a little time alone. You know, I want to kinda pray a little bit and meditate before I take my big walk. There're a couple of things I need to say to God." Tears welled in her eyes as she spoke, but she fought them, not wanting to ruin her make-up.

"You sure you're gonna be all right?" Erin asked, rubbing Micah's shoulders.

"Positive." Micah nodded slowly to assure her, then whispered, "Can you get everyone out of here for me since I'm confined to this chair for at least ten more minutes?" She wiggled her toes reminding Erin of her wet pedicure.

"Of course, sweetie," she agreed as she nudged away a tear from the corner of Micah's eye. "Don't start that or you are going to make all of us start." Erin stooped to wrap her arms around her. "I love you, girl."

Micah's eyes darted around the room in search of the clock, which displayed she had exactly three hours and fifteen minutes before the ceremony would begin. "I love you too," she nervously replied while a half smile crept across her face. Erin pulled away and began coaxing the girls out of the room, which started Micah's heart beating triple time.

"All right y'all, let's go! Micah needs some time alone with the Lord. We need to go down and make sure the reception hall is straight anyway."

The crew filed out of the room and headed to the lower level of the church where the reception would be held. Together the three ladies put the finishing touches on the room decorations and directed the caterers on where to set up. Rented pillars draped with white tulle and accented with fuchsia and teal flowers stood around the perimeter of the room. Each table had been draped with a white tablecloth and held beautiful candles settled inside footed hurricane vases clustered in sets of three and decorated with ribbon sleeves and the couple's monogram. The chair covers had been placed and a sweetheart table was elegantly positioned at the front of the room. Round teal paper lanterns with thin fuchsia ribbon trimming hung from the ceiling. Within ninety minutes, they had completed the room's transition from a blah fellowship hall to a classy reception hall with an upscale feel. Just as the ladies attempted to exit the room, the baker arrived with a wedding cake that featured five round tiers of white and chocolate cake iced in vanilla-amaretto-flavored frosting. Another forty-five minutes passed while the ladies watched in awe as the cake was set up. A band of teal fondant attached with fondant buttons wrapped around each tier, and white and fuchsia flowers topped off the cake, which towered at five feet tall.

"Everything is perfect; I guess we can get dressed now," Erin directed as they climbed the steps to the floor where the auxiliary rooms serving as dressing rooms were.

"You think I should tap on Micah's door and make sure she doesn't need anything?" Victori asked. "I bet she hasn't even cracked the door since we left."

"First of all, she asked to be left alone to pray; we have to respect that. Second, if she needed something, she would have called one of us. And third, why would she come out of the room for Rossi to see her? You know that's bad luck," Charvette chided.

"Well, I'll at least call her and see if she's all right." Just as the words left Erin's mouth, her cell phone vibrated against her hip, indicating an incoming text message. Erin flipped open her phone, thumbed to the message, and gasped out loud.

I left my headpiece in my bedroom closet!
Please go get it for me! Hurry!

"Oh my goodness," Erin exclaimed, noting the
time. "She left her headpiece at home! Somebody's going to have to go get it."

"What! Oh no." Victori glanced at her watch as
she shook her head. The ceremony was scheduled
to start in just an hour. "There is no way anybody
is gonna make it all the way to her house and back
and the wedding start on time."

"We're just going to have to stall it a few minutes. You know what they say about weddings
anyway: they always start late. I have her keys but
I still need to get dressed myself. Char, you go; you
know you drive like a bat out of hell . . . oops!
Sorry, Lord." Erin glanced apologetically up at the
ceiling while she dug Micah's keys out of the front
pocket of her jeans and handed them to Charvette. "I'll go let Rossi know what's going on."

Victori took off in one direction, while Erin
headed toward the small room the groomsmen
were crowded into. After a series of rapid knocks,
Rossi swung the door open, fully dressed minus
his jacket.

"It's time for us to head on down?" he asked,
grinning and rubbing his hands together nervously.

"Actually, you have a little more time than you
think," Erin began. "Micah left her headpiece,
and we had to send for it. That's going to delay
the ceremony by at least a half hour."

"That's no problem. I'm willing to wait as long
as it takes to marry Micah today. If the guests get
mad and go home, that's fine with me." Rossi

gazed with a half smile. "Just let us know when to go down."

"I sure will. Let me go slip into my dress."

"Yeah, 'cause I was just about to ask you did Micah kick you out of the wedding." He chuckled.

"No, we just had a few last-minute things to take care of. Speaking of, did you bring your checkbook? Give me the checks for the DJ, the pastor, and the videographer. I'm supposed to make sure they get their cut while you two get your honeymoon on."

"It sounds like you shoulda brought *your* checkbook then," he joked before disappearing into the room, then coming back with three labeled envelopes. He whistled as he handed them over. "You'd better tuck that all up here," he said as he ran his hand against his own chest. "Because that ain't no small piece of change in those envelopes."

"Whatever, Rossi. You act like this little bit of money is gonna break you. Micah shoulda tried to spend every dime you got."

"Oh trust me, she did!" he exclaimed. "But you know what, she's worth the wait and all the money she spent. We coulda flew to France three times for the price of this wedding."

Erin walked away giggling, then entered the room reserved as the dresing room for the female bridal party attendants.

"She ready yet?" Josephine asked as she turned toward Romni to have her zip her dress.

"She left her veil at the house. Charvette went to get it, so the wedding is going to start late."

"How in the world did she do that? That stuff should have been packed with her gown!" the rude wedding coordinator fussed. "Ain't you the maid of honor?" she asked Erin, pointing an acrylic nail her way. "You shole ain't on your job, 'cause you s''posed to had checked that for her!"

"And you s'posed to had taken better care of your teeth and you'd still have some instead of having that big ole black hole in the front of your face," Erin fired back.

"Who you thank you talkin' to?"

"Oh, sweetie, I don't have to think about it; I know exactly who I'm talking to. Now you already have a mess of tracks glued to your bald head. I suggest you stay over there before they end up on the floor and you'll have to direct this wedding in a head wrap!"

"Y'all calm down now. My nerves can't take all this," Josephine interjected, trying to diffuse the brewing confrontation. "This is my son's wedding day, and I don't want to see it messed up, so behave yo'self now," she spoke adamantly. "I didn't come all this way to see no catfight. God done spared my life and is allowing me to see my baby boy get married today, and I don't need nothing to ruin it."

The coordinator rolled her eyes and stormed out of the room.

Josephine looked toward Erin. "Now what you say is going on?"

Erin repeated the reason for the ceremony's delay once more while she slid into her dress. "We can play that photo slide show that Micah was going to play during the reception. That will at least give the guests something to see."

"It's better than nothing." Rossi's aunt said, with a shrug. "They can stand to see it twice, as long as some music is played in between. Let's see . . . if they wait until, like, five minutes after, then play a song, that's gonna take up ten minutes. Then show the video and play another song, that will be, like, seventeen, eighteen minutes, then play the video one more time for the people who will be rushing in at the last minute. By the time you do that and play one more song, hopefully Micah will be ready to go."

"That sounds like a plan to me," Erin commented. "Let me run down to the sound booth and see if I can get that set up." She reached into her bridesmaid's goody bag and pulled out a copy of the DVD that Micah would give to all her attendants. "I'll be right back." After sliding her feet into a pair of slippers, she scooted out the door with her cell phone in tow. She dialed Micah's number to let her know what was going on. Micah picked up on the first ring.

"Hey, princess," Erin cooed.

"I am sooo sorry," Micah began.

"Don't worry about it. Charvette should be back in about twenty minutes, and in the meantime, I'm going to have the audio crew run the video you were planning to show during the reception to buy some time. Is that okay? It's the only thing we could think of to not make the late start seem so late and tacky."

"Ooh! Great idea! See, that's why you're the maid of honor. Thank you, girl," Micah sighed in relief. "When Charvette gets back, can you help me get into my dress?"

"Of course, shug. I'd be honored to."

Charvette arrived twenty minutes later, then shimmied into her gown. "All right, let's go down here and get the queen in her dress." After securing their purses and doing final mirror checks, the team of women sashayed toward Micah's room.

Erin knocked. "Mrs. Evans," she sang, "it's almost time." There was no response. "Micah, open the door. We want to see you and make sure you're looking right for your man. Stop playing and waiting until the last minute!" When there was no answer the second time, an uneasy expression began to cross the ladies' faces simultaneously.

"Sweetie, open up," Victori called as she rattled her knuckles against the door one more time. Slowly her eyes stretched with panic.

"Something's not right," Erin concluded, twisting the knob. "We need to try to find somebody with a key. Victori, you go downstairs and see how full the church is." She attempted to turn the doorknob again as she gave directives. "Micah?" she called one last time. "Go around to the outside door, Charvette. Maybe it's unlocked."

A few minutes later, Charvette opened the door from the inside and let Erin into the empty room. "She ain't in here," Charvette announced, shaking her head. "This girl 'bout to make me sweat my deodorant off!"

The two ladies looked around the room in a confused panic. Shortly Victori joined them.

"It's so many people in this church you would think it was Easter Sunday," she announced. "Where's Micah?"

"We're trying to figure that out," Erin responded.

"What?!"

"What is this?" Erin asked rhetorically, taking note of two envelopes that had been posted across the mirror and Micah's three-carat diamond ring sitting in its original box on top of the vanity. One of the envelopes had the three ladies' names written across the front, while the other was labeled "Read This Last." Erin snatched them down and took a seat on the dressing room sofa. She ripped through the seal of the one addressed to the women and unfolded the letter.

> *Erin, Charvette, and Victori,*
> *I know this comes as a surprise for everyone, but I will not marry Rossi today. Several months ago I realized that he simply was not the man for me, and because you are my best girlfriends, you know the details. Unfortunately, it just wasn't there for Rossi and me and I had to let him go. But before I did, I had to figure out a way to beat him at his own game. I will see you when I return in a few weeks.*
> *Love you!*
> *Micah*
> *P.S.: Once you have read the second letter, please seal it in a new envelope that I've left on the vanity and ensure that Rossi gets it along with his ring. And, Erin, there is no baby . . . never was.*

"What? She was pregnant?" Victori blurted.

"Wow," Charvette started. "I can't believe she did this."

"And this wedding wasn't cheap either," Victori exclaimed. "I'm glad she paid for these dresses! Hurry up and open that other letter."

Erin held her breath as she tore through the remaining sealed envelope.

They all gasped in shock as they read the letter Jaison Anthony McDonald had written to Rossi.

Three hours earlier . . .

As soon as the door was shut, Micah leapt to her feet and ensured it was locked tight. In a matter of seconds her towel pooled at her feet as she rushed around the room in the buff in search of her overnight bag. Someone had done her the favor of tossing it in a corner and piling her things on top of it, making it a little bit of a challenge to find. She glanced at the clock again, taking note that two minutes had passed.

Quickly, Micah dug out a pair of bikini briefs and a sports bra, pulled them both on, tugged on her jeans and slipped into a pink T-shirt that read "I am famous on MySpace," then jammed her feet into a pair of socks and her favorite Sketchers, hoisted her bag on her shoulder, dug her keys out of the side, and tiptoed down the back hallway and out the back door. Cautiously she peeked both ways before darting to her truck, then dove inside and took off.

Once she felt she was a comfortable distance from the church, she slid a CD into the player, nudged the search button until she reached the last track, then blasted Frankie Beverly's "Before I Let Go," and sped to Richmond International Airport, headed for Montego Bay, Jamaica.

It was six in the morning three days later when Micah peeled her eyes open and found herself still nestled in her husband's arms. Feeling her stir, he awoke and leaned in to plant kisses on her shoulders. Instinctively, Micah moaned, reminiscing on the intimate sunset ceremony on the beach where they'd exchanged vows just hours before and spent the night making passionate love.

"Good morning, baby," he whispered before landing a gentle kiss beneath her earlobe.

"Yeah, it is, isn't it?" She smiled, turning her head slightly to peck his lips.

"Every morning will be a beautiful morning as long as I have you here in my arms."

Micah fully turned her body toward him, pressing her breasts against his bare chest, and wrapping her arm around his torso. "And every night will be incredible as long as you make love to me like you did last night."

"I don't have to wait until it's nighttime, do I, baby?" he asked.

She let her body answer for her as she traced a line up the side of his calf, knee, and thigh with her big toe. He caught her leg in the crook of his arm, then skillfully slid into her body, causing her head to drift backward.

"My wife, my wife," he chanted softly as he kissed her over and over again. "My beautiful, loving, wonderful, sexy wife," he continued, gently thrusting between each word. Micah called his name over and over until they both reached a euphoric climax and collapsed in each other's arms.

"I believe you owe me breakfast," Micah exhaled as she drew her shoulders up and let a smile cross her face.

"You're right," Stephen chuckled and kissed his wife once more. "I did say that I would serve my wife breakfast in bed, didn't I? And I would but I've already planned for room service to arrive with our breakfast right . . . about . . . now."

As if the concierge had been standing outside the door of their suite, there was a light tapping. Stephen leapt to his feet and threw on a robe before allowing the server in with a cart. Once the delectable array of fresh fruits, flaky croissants, crème-filled crepes, and fresh juice and coffee was laid out, the server handed Stephen a small folio requiring his signature. Quickly Stephen dug through a small carry-on in search of a pen, pulling out a handful of items and dropping them on a small table. Included in those items was his handheld pen scanner that still had Jaison's letter saved to its memory. . . .

Visit Kimberly online at:
www.myspace.com/perfectshoe
and at
www.myspace.com/kimberlytmatthews